Robyn Leslie

aND

THe TRail Of CLUeS

SUGAR DUCKY
BOOKS, INC.

Florida Writers Association
1st Place Award Winner

Published by
Sugar Ducky Books, Inc
P.O. Box 56954
Jacksonville, Fl 32241-6954
http://www.sugarduckybooks.com

Attention Educational Institutions: A teacher's manual is available.
Contact your local supply store or Sugar Ducky Books, Inc.

Cover art Copyright © Laura Hartinger
Illustrations by Laura Hartinger

The following trademarks appear in this book: Coca-Cola, Tootsie Pops,
Blow Pop, Hershey Cocoa, Converse Chuck Taylor All Star Shoes

Printed in Canada

Publisher's - Cataloging-In-Publication Data

Leslie, Robyn.
    Rinny and the trail of clues / Robyn Leslie. --p. cm.
    SUMMARY : Erin Olson enters the 5th grade presidential
    race only to discover her opponent is the class clown
    and one of the smartest kids around. And what does the
    mysterious note tucked into her desk mean?
    LCCN 2002116981
    ISBN 0-9727388-8-6

    1. Elections--Juvenile fiction.
    2. Schools--Junvenile fiction.
    [1. Elections--Fiction. 2. Schools--Fiction.
    3. Mystery and detective stories.] I. Title.

PZ7.L562626Rin 2003   [Fic]
                    QBI33-1172

For
Erin, her friend Sean Lowe,
and my husband Gary

Table of Contents

The Message   9

Books are words
that come from the heart,
Help the imagination,
Make the brain think,
And let you go far beyond places
no one can think of.

Chelsea Mayes, age 9

The Message

Beware! Someone you know will lead you down a long, mysterious path. Choose your path wisely or you may not reach the end. Trust no one.

The black splotchy letters stretched unevenly across the small crumpled note. Erin's heart hesitated as she read the note again in the privacy of her living room. The neatly folded paper had been tucked inside her desk at school today. It was a haunting message. With furrowed brow, she paced back and forth across the wooden floor. Only Billy Perez, the most brilliant troublemaker in the entire school and king of the class clowns, would send such a note. And the unsigned message had appeared after the teacher had announced that Erin and Billy were the two candidates running in the class presidential race.

Erin stopped to pull the note closer. Her long brown ponytail fell loosely across the scribbled words as her large hazel eyes combed every letter. There wasn't anything unusual about the mysterious paper. Of course, she didn't expect a signature, but some kind of clue would have been nice. She held her breath as she stared at the message. Someone wanted to scare her away from the race, she decided after a long sigh. And that was really annoying, because she was born to be president.

Closing her eyes, she envisioned her new opponent. The dark, curly hair on top of Billy's head barely reached her chin when he stood next to her. Erin was the tallest student in the fifth-grade, but that didn't seem to bother him. Just this morning he had placed a wad of gum on the back of her chair while grinning innocently. Billy Perez dipped pencils into glue bottles and passed them out to unsuspecting victims. He made paper airplanes out of spelling tests, coughed constantly during silent reading, burped nonstop in the cafeteria, and drew faces on knees that pretended to talk. And just last weekend, he had tried rollerblading off the school roof. Erin tried to muffle her cry of anguish as she returned the folded note to her pocket. This boy was also one of the smartest kids around.

The house was quiet with the television off and grandfather upstairs resting his eyes. Backed up against the front of the couch, Erin sat Indian style on the living room floor with her art supplies. After applying the last dab of carefully placed paint, she stood to read her masterpiece. After all, posters were hung on walls, away from the reader, so she stepped back. This was her first project as a presidential candidate, and she wanted it to be perfect. *Vote for Erin Olson*, the poster shouted in bold shades of pink and orange fluorescent paint. At least she hoped it shouted. But the more she looked at it, the more she worried.

This poster was important. It was supposed to grab your attention. It was supposed to stick in your mind. But she wasn't sure this was the image she wanted stuck in others' minds. She looked again and groaned. Even the bright orange and pink balloon letters didn't change the fact that it was plain. It was more than drab—it was pitiful. And, as if everyone didn't already use the word *boring* over and over again, now she would have to say it, too.

Billy would be a very tough opponent and she would have to concentrate on being the best. But writing a slogan for a poster was supposed to be easy. At least it seemed easy for everyone else, but she couldn't think of anything clever. *Say No to Billy the Silly* was terrible, and *Olson is Wholesome* was worse. She needed something really cool, something all the students would understand. Something like *Things Go Better With Coke,* a slogan that, now that she thought about it, probably took weeks to write. She had only tonight! Sighing loudly, she slumped down to the floor alongside the poster.

"So, you were really picked to run for president, huh, Rinny?" teased the tall, slim, athletic boy stepping through the screen door opening.

Erin turned and smiled at her best friend, Temple Black. She knew he would help with Billy. A year older, and a sixth-grader, Temple was head of his class. And he had won a national award in math, beating out lots of students in the next county. Plus he had designed, built, and launched a rocket all by himself. His super-duper-stream-lined-turbo-rocket had climbed straight up in the sky and disappeared from sight. The watching crowd had squealed when it did that. A front-page picture of him bowing to the people had appeared in the paper the next day.

Girls loved Temple and thought he was cute, but Erin didn't understand why. His brown eyes and long, dark eyelashes looked like spiders under his wire-framed glasses. His chin had a dimple in the middle, and he only combed his black, wavy hair once a day. When it was windy outside, he looked like a madman the rest of the day. Her mother thought he was very handsome, but to Erin, Temple just looked like Temple: the boy with the large grin.

She tapped one of the markers with her foot. "I'm running against Billy Perez," she sighed.

"Really? 'Billy the Terrible' is your opponent? That's awful! He has a whole army of sneaky friends. They'll be right beside him making trouble. Tell me, My Lady, what can I do to be of service?" he said with a low bow.

Temple fancied himself a knight in shining armor and loved to bow. Erin ignored him. She was used to it. Shoving the markers out of her way, she realized how bothered she was that Billy and his rambunctious friends were against her. She pulled the note from her pocket and placed it in Temple's hand.

"Read this, and stop calling me 'Rinny.' That was my name when I was little, but I'm not a little girl anymore. My name is Erin. It means peace."

"Sure. Anything you say, Rin," Temple said nonchalantly. He studied the note with amusement. "Aw, he's just bluffing. He'll probably push you down on the ground at recess, just to make you mad. Now, tell me all about the campaign. He'll be really sorry when you win. Besides, you and I are a team, sort of like the Three Musketeers, only we're a twosome. What he does to you, he also does to me."

Erin smiled affectionately. "I'm working on my poster. My teacher, Mrs. Brambles, says a poster is supposed to capture everything a person stands for, but in a simple way. You know, like an advertisement."

Temple looked at the poster with a puzzled look. "And you think *Vote for Erin Olson* tells your story?"

"I know," she groaned, wringing her hands. "I've been thinking and thinking of what to say. But my mind is totally blank. And I do want to tell the students to vote for me."

"Boy, 'simple' is definitely the key word, Rin," he said teasingly. "*Waaay* too simple. But I do like the pink and orange colors. Everyone knows pink is your favorite color, so I guess that part tells a story."

She picked up the poster and held her head back, squinting at the words. A faint knock rapped in the background.

"Someone's at the front door, Rin," Temple quipped. "Want me to get it, Your Majesty?"

"I didn't hear the doorbell," she said distantly, putting down her poster and looking at it again. Pink was her favorite color, but she wasn't sure it made a good poster. Her mother had pointed out that bright colors were used in the old hippie shops around the college. They were the shops her mother had loved when she was in school. Those shops used every color invented. No one missed someone wearing a bright orange-purple-hot-pink-electric-blue-sunshine-yellow tie-died shirt.

"Someone knocked, Rinny," he said again. "Should I get it?"

Shrugging her shoulders, she walked over to the screen door. "No one's there," she said, turning back toward her project. "Besides, I'm not expecting anyone."

"But, I heard footsteps on the porch," Temple insisted.

Opening the door, Erin checked the driveway, the sidewalks, and the yards. The streets were completely empty, except for Teddy, her black cat. An angry bumblebee hovered above his head as he raced across the yard. Erin giggled as he frantically twitched in midair. "Nope, no one there," she stated again.

Something drew her eyes down as she was closing the door—something inches from her foot. She gasped and, after blinking several times, stared at the motionless object. Lying dead across the doormat was a rat the size of a small cat. Tied to its neck was a red ribbon. A stifled scream caught in her throat as she froze in place, her eyes fixed on the dark form. Temple moved her aside with a sharp poke in the back. He choked when he saw the creature.

Curiosity finally overcame Erin's hesitation, and she stooped down for a closer look. A small piece of paper had been tucked under the red bow. The rat's swollen tongue stuck out between pointed teeth. Leaping back into the house, she slammed the door shut. "Yuck!" she squealed with a shiver.

"Maybe it's a birthday present from Billy," Temple said eerily.

"My birthday isn't for two more weeks," she protested, wiping her hands repeatedly against her sweater. "Besides, how would Billy know it was my birthday? I haven't told anyone at school."

She stared anxiously at the front door before opening it again. Temple looked off in a different direction, tapping his chin with an index finger. "Then perhaps the competition has left you a message," he said with a soft whisper.

"What do you mean?" she asked, looking down at the hideous lump with a tongue.

"I don't know," he said, throwing his hands up into the air. "I'm just guessing here. What do you think it could be? After all, Rinny, it is your house and your doormat and now your rat. It appears you'll have to examine it."

"I don't think so." She clamped her eyes shut and slid her hands into her pockets. "No way."

"Okay," said Temple, "I'll get a broom and just scoop it into the trash, and that will be the end of it. Then we'll never know what this whole thing was about." He started for the kitchen.

"No, wait," she sighed, opening her eyes. After lifting her feet carefully over the doormat, she stepped onto the porch. Temple followed with a quick jump, making a thump as he hit the floor. His wire-framed glasses fell halfway down his nose. He squatted next to Erin, and they stared at the rat together.

"Temple, I don't like this. Someone has just put a dead rat on my doorstep, and I don't know why." She poked the motionless body with a marker. "This is creepy. I'm calling Grandpa. He'll get rid of it."

"No, wait Rinny," Temple cautioned. "We need to see what this piece of paper is, don't we? You've always said you love a mystery. I mean, there was a reason someone did this. I say we check the rat first and then decide what to do."

"Okay," she said slowly, wanting to call grandfather anyway. He would find the person responsible for the dead rat. Her grandpa wouldn't put up with someone putting dead rats on the porch. He would march Billy Perez back to the house, make him get rid of it properly and then expect an apology, campaign or no campaign.

Temple reached into his pocket and retrieved a pocketknife to snip the paper free. "It looks like a note," he said, handing it over.

She unfolded the tightly wadded paper. "It says, 'Meet me alone, at the old maple tree in the cemetery. If you don't respond, I will poison the ducks at the pond.'"

Erin looked away in horror. She loved the ducks. She and Grandfather saved all their leftover bread for trips to the pond. The ducks would gobble every morsel. And every spring there were new ducklings to watch. She loved to see their small tails standing straight up in the water as they dove for food. She knew each duck by heart.

"I don't understand," Erin exclaimed. "Meet who alone? And why would anyone want to hurt Fred and Ethel . . . and their babies?"

Temple shook his head back and forth. "I don't know. But I would sure hate to see it happen. You'd better go. I'll go too, if you want me to."

Erin stared angrily at the words. First, someone sticks a spooky note inside her desk at school and then drops a rotting rat on her front porch. Now she finds a note threatening to hurt the ducks. It wasn't fair. She didn't want to go. Her shoulders drooped in despair. Everyone in town loved the ducks, including her. And threatening helpless animals was mean. What did the ducks have to do with the campaign? They had never harmed anyone. Stamping her foot on the ground, she folded her arms in protest. This was dirty politics. Billy Perez was going too far.

"You know, Rinny," said Temple, "we could take this note to the police and let them worry about the ducks. Then you wouldn't have to go to the cemetery."

"But, I need to know who is causing all this trouble," she said, trying to sound brave. "And if I don't go to the cemetery, something else might be hurt. And what if the police aren't able to stop the ducks from being poisoned? I would never be able to look at the pond again."

"So, what are you trying to say?" queried Temple.

Erin's arms unfolded as her anger melted away. She hesitated, chewing nervously on her lower lip. It was scary to think of the cemetery at night. The autumn sun set early and the cemetery was far from the town lights. Her foot tapped uneasily against the pine floor. After a long sigh, she mustered a small smile and threw Temple his jacket. "Grandfather would say, 'Presidents don't run at the first sign of trouble.' Let's go."

iNTO THE CEMETERY

The evening sun was slowly sinking below the treetops. Erin glanced behind her shoulder as she and Temple made their way into the big cemetery. Old, weathered gravestones stood guard over the green grass that now covered the graves. Deep into the grounds, at the farthest end actually, stood the old maple tree, planted in a section of the cemetery dating back to the 1700s. Her great, great, great, great grandfather Snook was laid to rest there.

Legend said he was a pirate. He had served as a first mate aboard a privateer ship, sailing back and forth over the seas. But the legend told of the ship's captain taking a portion of the money for hauling slaves from the African coast. The captain, paid handsomely for his cargo and always looking for ways to advance himself, boarded more slaves than anyone thought humanly possible. Chaining them into small spaces, he cut both their food and fresh water rations.

Great Grandfather Snook spoke against this practice, only to find himself an outcast among the seafaring crew. He felt it was better to steal from the rich than make blood money from the unfortunate, as he called them. So the tale goes that Great Grandfather left the merchants to become the notorious Captain Snook of the pirate ship Red Dog. Over her great, great, great, great grandfather's bones lay a simple stone marker that read, "Captain Benjamin Snook, Gentleman Pirate, exiled from England, 1697." Erin thought it was odd that her note said go to the same location.

They stopped at a fork in the road. Several paths weaved in and out of the vast grounds. They could see the old maple tree at the farthest end. From where they stood, they would be able to see anyone coming or going.

"Let's stop here for a minute," Erin said thoughtfully, before setting her father's heavy Coleman lantern on the ground. The fingers on her right hand were imprinted with a deep groove from the thin metal handle. She planned on lighting the lantern once the sun went down. Its bright white rays would make everything within twenty feet visible.

Temple walked among the gravestones, reading names and dates, while Erin checked the small envelope tucked inside her pocket. Inside the envelope was her secret weapon. Of course, she knew most people wouldn't think of it as a weapon, but she did. She knew it would be useful when the time came. But until then, it would ride safely inside her pocket.

"Hey Rin," called Temple from a graveside, "did you know there was a skunk named Jane buried next to an Otis Jones? This old trapper had a skunk for a wife, and they both died from the fever and were buried together."

Erin scrunched up her nose.

Temple laughed. "Ha! You fell for it. That was a joke, Rinny. You've been way too serious since we left the house," he said, returning to where they had stopped in the road.

Ignoring him and deep in thought, Erin picked up the lantern with her other hand. "Maybe you'd better go down the other side," she said. "We shouldn't be together in case someone's watching. The note said to come alone. You can hide behind the Wadesworth marker. It's between the two paths."

"I don't know, Rinny," he said slowly. "I'll be too far away if you get into trouble. Those trees are pretty skinny. They won't hide me."

"I'll be all right Temple. Billy might be a troublemaker, but he won't hurt me. I have to catch him if I can. I'll automatically win if I catch him. I hope he knows that."

Temple looked concerned. "Did it ever occur to you that maybe it isn't Billy?"

She started to say no, then hesitated. Of course it was Billy. It couldn't be anyone else. Nothing like this had ever happened before. Dead rats didn't drop onto doorsteps . . . and Billy was just the sort of person to do such a thing. Once, in school, he had brought in a smashed bullfrog. Then he had placed it inside his neighbor's desk and waited for the boy to come in. The boy had stuck his hand into the desk, discovered the frog and, after seeing the squashed guts oozing from his hand, had fallen over backwards in his chair. Billy's eyes had beamed.

Up until now, she had attended school, done her homework and played with her friends. She had never given Billy a hard time. But Billy had underestimated her. Yes, the rat was creepy, but it would take more than a dead rat to make her back away from being president. And Temple was on her side. There wasn't anyone smarter than he.

A twig snapped in the distance, and she turned. "Go," she hissed before running off. "I'll scream if there's trouble."

Not only was the maple tree at the very farthest edge of the cemetery, it was bordered by thick woods and a nearby farm. The tree had been planted when the senior Wadesworth died in 1700. Now the ground under the tree was bare, the gnarled roots running along the dirt, starving out the plant life. The trunk was enormous, and Erin nestled up against its base. The giant stood over her, it's wide branches spreading out like a mother welcoming her children home. An owl hooted nearby.

The sun had slipped below the horizon. With matches in hand, Erin lifted the glass globe from the lantern. A sudden explosion of white light burst from the mantle. Shadows danced across the road as she replaced the globe. It was as if the sun had not gone down. She held the lantern high, searching the grounds. Long, thin shadows stretched out from the arched headstones. She looked up among the thick branches, then along the path just taken. Looking to the left, then to the right, she saw only dancing shadows. The place was empty.

She waited. What if this person didn't show up? she wondered. Maybe this was a wild goose chase. Maybe this was a joke. Maybe Billy and his friends were hiding behind the headstones, laughing as she jumped with each tiny sound.

Tomorrow was the day she and Billy were to give their speeches. She hadn't thought about what to say, and here she was, huddled under an old tree in the dark, waiting for someone who wasn't here. Her watch showed 7:30. She would only wait ten minutes. If Billy didn't show up before then, she would leave. She had been a fool already.

For what seemed like a long time, she waited, listening. The sound of the hissing lantern was all that filled the air. Moths circled the glass globe, diving into the hot glass and bouncing off. A branch snapped. She jumped to her feet, positioning her back against the massive tree trunk. Scream for Temple, echoed inside her head.

She placed a hand over her mouth instead. Screaming would be the wrong thing to do. The person might run off, and she had to know who it was. Bending slightly away from the tree, she reached for the lantern.

Something grabbed her from behind. She twisted and turned, trying to see the attacker, but couldn't. Crumpled paper covered her face as the strong arm that was wrapped around her pinned her arms. Large pieces of tape bit against her skin as the roll went round and round, sealing the paper shut. She blinked but was lost in darkness. Her hands strained to grab at the paper grocery bag enclosing her head. She screamed but realized that the sound, so loud inside the bag, was muffled under the heavy weight of the paper.

Her attacker wrestled her, face down, to the ground. She tried pushing up, but a heavy body sat on her back, knocking the wind out of her. She opened her mouth to scream again but couldn't find the air. Struggling under the weight, she tried screaming in short puffs but they sounded more like groans than screams. Her arms were twisted behind her back and taped together at the wrists. She couldn't break the hold. Putting her feet together, she tried kicking into the person's back. Her thrusts met empty air, and she still couldn't catch her breath to call for help.

THREE

THE MYSTERY BEGINS

Erin struggled, her right cheek flattened against the bag's smooth surface. The person sitting on her back held her head to the ground. Both wrists tied behind her back left her helpless. The person on top had the advantage. She continued to kick backwards into the air. Unable to breathe freely, she swallowed small amounts of air. "Temple . . . " she mouthed breathlessly, "please hear me . . . I need you."

Suddenly, the pressure was gone. A long stream of fresh air entered her lungs, allowing her to catch her breath. The weight had mysteriously lifted from the aching muscles of her back. Kicking wildly, she rolled over and sat up expecting to be knocked down again, but she wasn't. She listened quietly to the sound of hurried footsteps on the run. The footsteps soon disappeared, and she stumbled to her feet.

"Rinny! Rinny!" yelled Temple, his voice growing closer. "Are you all right?"

She struggled, trying to break the tape around her wrists. "Help me, Temple," she called out with what she knew was a muffled voice.

Temple stopped in front of her and laughed. "Okay, Okay," he sputtered in amusement. "Stop moving . . . or I won't be able to help you. I wish I had a camera. You should see what you look like. You're all covered in dirt, and there's a face drawn on the paper bag. One googly eye is pointing up and the other one is pointing down. The mouth has fat lips that look like two tires stacked on top of each other. This would make a great picture for your poster—*Miss Erin Olson, Your Fifth-grade President.*"

She winced when he abruptly pulled the tape from her neck. He lifted the paper bag up and grinned at the scowling face underneath. He was clearly delighted.

"I didn't see who it was," she said, angrily motioning to her taped hands. His pocketknife cut the bindings. "The dirty sneak attacked me from behind, then taped this grocery bag over my head. I tried calling you, but you didn't answer me." Erin glared at the silly expression on his face. "What's so funny? Someone just attacked me!"

"Were you hurt?" he asked calmly.

"Of course I was hurt," she replied indignantly.

"Have you been cut or bruised in any way? Did the person hit you? Were you kicked, or bitten or poked? Were you strangled or mangled? Have you been shot?" he asked calmly again.

"No, no, no, no, no, no," she said to each question. "I was bagged."

"Bagged?" he exclaimed. "Does that hurt?"

"Of course not," she said, now laughing. She ran her fingers slowly through her hair. "Okay, I wasn't really hurt but the person was stronger than me. He sat on my back and taped my hands together. It had to be a boy, because he wasn't heavy like a man but he was stronger than a girl. I didn't see him, and he didn't say anything. Not one word that I could recognize. He must have seen you coming, because he jumped off."

"I don't think the person really wanted to hurt you," he said, holding the paper bag up in the air, with his hand sticking out the top. "This bag has a hole in the top for breathing. And this tape is only thin masking tape. These aren't the tools of a hardened criminal. Maybe he just wanted to scare you."

Erin looked over the bag, moving her fingers in and out of the hole. She frowned at the animated face drawn on the front. It looked like England's Mr. Blobby, the pink character with crazy eyes. "You don't bring these things if you are just talking. He must have planned on tying me up from the very beginning. This was the plan all along. "

"I believe you are right, my dear," Temple said with an air of authority. Then he brushed the dirt from her shoulders. "But what would prompt someone do such a thing? And for what purpose? We still don't know anything. The mystery is still a mystery."

"Well, tomorrow I'm going to ask Billy Perez why he did this. I want to see the expression on his face when I tell him we know it's him," she said. After picking up the lantern she checked to make sure her secret weapon had survived the attack. Then, holding Temple's hand, she raised the lantern high and led them away from the dark, eerie shadows of the cemetery at night. The rustling of the wind, and the howling of strange sounds, no longer concerned her. And she smiled when the barn owl hooted once again. Billy Perez had not beaten her tonight.

FOUR

THE SPEECH

Standing outside the school door, Erin yawned. The alarm had gone off, and she couldn't believe it had been time to get up. It seemed as if she had barely gone to sleep. Today's speech had taken forever to write last night, and when she finally did fall asleep, a hairy monster with the body of a bear and the face of a man attacked her in her dreams. Every time she stood to give her speech, the monster would push her down. Its twisted body would dance and laugh after doing its dirty deed. Over and over she fell. Finally, she remained on the cold ground and recited her speech from memory. The squirrels jeered and threw acorns. The birds cackled in the trees. The dancing monster clapped with furry paws.

Last night, she wanted to tell Grandfather about the rat and the cemetery, but Temple convinced her not to be so hasty. Things might change if they told someone, and they needed to solve the mystery first. And if it was Billy, she needed to catch him before the election. She needed to expose him for the sneak that he is before the final vote for president.

Her watch showed five minutes before the morning bell. A crowd of children filled the front walk of the school. They poured out of the school buses and cars now pulling up to the curb. She didn't know whether to watch the school bus or the sidewalks for Billy Perez. Up until now, she had tried to avoid him. She dreaded talking to him alone. He was so unpredictable.

The other day, when Mrs. Brambles had announced Billy's excellent report on American Presidents, Erin had turned to see two pencils sticking out of his nose like walrus tusks. How could she talk to someone like that? It was even more puzzling how he knew all the answers. Mrs. Brambles would ask a question so hard that all the other students would hide by slumping down in their chairs. But Billy, who had been folding his homework into paper cubes, would raise his hand and give the correct answer.

Now her watch reported three minutes before the morning bell. A car pulled up to the curb, and the passenger door swung open. Erin sunk back. Out stepped grouchy Charlotte Pillman, the very last person on earth she wanted to see. She slid behind the large cement pillar. Fortunately, if she turned sideways, the pillar was perfect for hiding. And she wasn't in the mood to face Charlotte, the bully of the fifth-grade class.

This was the girl who hated her. This was the girl who loathed her. This was the girl who snapped her pencils in two . . . who tipped the contents of her desk out and left footprints on her coat. It was bad enough to wait for Billy, but it was even worse to encounter Charlotte Pillman. She peered cautiously around the edge of the smooth, white surface.

"Charlotte, I'm talking to you," screamed a raspy voice from inside the car.

Charlotte turned her back to the open window.

"Listen, you little brat," continued the female voice from inside the car, "If you ever give me that snotty look again, I'll slap your ugly face even harder. And I'll enjoy it. You think you're too good for your family? You think you're too good to take care of your brother and sisters and your grandma and grandpa?

"I don't care if you do have homework. You're supposed to do that in school, and if your teacher has a problem with that, I'll just set her straight . . . stupid teachers, not doing their jobs at school and expecting the kids to learn it on their own time at night. When you get home, you have chores to do, and if they ain't done, I'll boot you right out on the street. We'll see how you like sleeping with your homeless buddies down by the river. Ha! Ha! You hear me—right out on the street . . . "

The school bell rang. Charlotte walked through the school door without looking back. The woman's voice could no longer be heard over the deafening noise. Astounded, Erin watched Charlotte disappear into the building. Glancing nervously at her watch, she stooped down to look inside the car. It was time to go in, but she had to see this person.

A small, skinny woman with hair that looked like it had been sucked up with a vacuum cleaner fumbled with a foot-long cigarette. Dark roots grew out from under the many-shades-of-yellow hair. She balanced the bent cigarette on her lower lip. Her unsteady hand tried aligning a match with the crooked tip. After taking two long drags, she popped a piece of chewing gum into her mouth. Like a cow chewing its cud, she moved the cigarette to the corner of her mouth, flicked the gum wrapper out the window, stomped on the gas pedal, and made an illegal U-turn out of the driveway.

Erin's mouth dropped open. No wonder Charlotte Pillman was so grouchy. Anyone would be grouchy, living with a person like that. The poor thing didn't deserve the title "grouchy Charlotte" anymore. She was poor Charlotte. Poor Charlotte Pillman. Erin would never look at poor Charlotte Pillman the same way again.

Running up the stairs two at a time, Erin raced through the classroom door, dropped her poster on the teacher's desk, and emptied her backpack before the tardy bell rang. Billy Perez smiled as he made his way to the back row. And Billy's sparkling eyes always meant trouble. Last time she had seen that look, the principal had just caught Billy placing a lit cigarette into the mouth of George Washington's statue.

Her neighbor, Charlotte, was looking straight ahead. Normally, Erin would be happy to see Charlotte looking away, but today Charlotte was scowling more than usual. It was time for the homework monitor to collect the papers, and Charlotte had placed her finished homework on top of the desk—but the paper was completely blank. Only her name appeared at the top. Erin looked down at her own homework, the synonyms due for spelling and the extra report on nineteenth century toys, for Social Studies. The report had taken two weeks to research and illustrate with colored pencils. She never realized how lucky she was to have a grandpa who walked her to the library and checked her work.

Erin sat up and cleared her throat. "You look very pretty today, Charlotte." But as soon as the words left her lips, she gulped, wishing she could take them back. Charlotte's clothes looked like she had slept in them for a week. Her uncombed stringy hair stuck to her head like a glove. Long, pointy strands of dirty hair fell down into her eyes. The tongues on her filthy sneakers stuck straight up, and the untied shoestrings lay across the floor.

"Are you making fun of me, Miss Perfect? You think you're funny," she snapped with a growl. "We can't all be like you."

Erin sank down in her chair, trying to avoid the laser-beam stare. Charlotte's steely eyes were fixed on her like a target. The sharp penetrating beams were hitting her with streams of molten hot lava. One after the other, they came, never letting up. She looked down, pretending awkwardly to clean her fingernails. Next time she would look before giving out a compliment—especially to poor Charlotte.

Mrs. Brambles positioned herself in the middle of the room and held up the two campaign posters. Erin had folded her poster to fit inside her backpack. Grandpa had suggested rolling it up and carrying it in her hand, but she thought it might fall victim to someone like Billy in the hallway. He might have grabbed it as she walked by.

She looked over the two posters. The crumpled one with the frayed edges belonged to her. *Vote for Erin Olson,* it said simply. The perfectly straight poster belonged to Billy. It said, *Billy Perez Cares* in large letters across the top and *Billy Perez for President,* across the bottom. Erin blinked, and looked again at the side-by-side posters. Billy's poster was the real thing. Twice as large as hers, his school photograph covered the entire background. And printed in large movie screen letters were the words *Billy Perez Cares, Billy Perez for President.* It looked like a poster straight from a campaign headquarters.

Saddened, she stared at her scrawny and pitiful work. All four edges had been crushed in, thanks to her books smashing it back and forth in her backpack. And the extra paint added to it this morning had run down the sides of the balloon letters. They looked like dripping candles. She sat up and glared at Billy Perez. Someone had drawn a little smiley face inside the "O" in *Vote* on her poster, and had placed two horns on top.

"What a stupid-looking poster," whispered Charlotte. "What do you want to be? The class cheerleader, line monitor, or really bad artist? Hey, how about school dummy?"

Erin turned away from the death-ray eyes and slumped down in her chair. She didn't feel very well. Charlotte laughed out loud. Erin glanced at the posters again. Mrs. Brambles was right. Billy's poster was talking to all the people, telling them he cared. His message was personal. He told them directly that he was running for president. And with his picture in the background, they wouldn't forget his face every time they thought of a person for president. She was tempted to vote for him, herself. He had a powerful poster. She put her head down on the desk to hide.

"Okay class, now let's hear from our two candidates. Are you prepared, Erin?" asked Mrs. Brambles cheerfully.

"I guess so," Erin whispered shyly. She removed the paper sticking out of the top of her pocket. Thinking it might get lost, she had checked her pocket four times before leaving the house and three times on the way to school. Things had a way of getting lost.

She unfolded the paper carefully, stood up straight and looked directly at the students—just the way Grandfather had taught her. Everyone was staring back. Even Billy was giving her his undivided attention. No computer toys, no tapping on the table with his pencil, no wild-eyed winks. Mrs. Brambles had taken a seat at the back of the class with a notebook in hand, and the principal had come through the front door to join her.

Then Erin remembered the hat. She opened the bag she had brought from home, and lifted out the foot-tall, rainbow-striped hat-of-many-colors and placed it on her head. Willing her hands not to shake, she cleared her throat and started with a strong, firm voice, "Good morning Ladybugs and Jellybeans."

A wave of puzzled faces crossed the room. No one smiled. There was no laughter—just blank stares. A frown crossed the principal's face. Mrs. Brambles raised an eyebrow. Charlotte let out a loud snicker. Crossing two fingers behind her back, Erin gripped the paper nervously with her other hand and started the introduction again.

"Welcome Ladybugs and Jellybeans!
I now stand before you, to sit behind you,
To tell you something I know nothing about.
Tomorrow on Good Friday, which will be Saturday,

There will be a ladies meeting that only men can attend,
Free Admission to all, please pay at the door,
There'll be seats all around, please sit on the floor,
Free Parking in rear, please pay the cashier,
I'm glad you all came, but I wish you weren't here."

"What?" blurted out Tom, the redhead in the second row.

The students looked at each other in confusion. Billy smirked and nudged the boy next to him. Mrs. Brambles whispered something to the principal. Erin looked at the poster pinned up on the board. The words *Vote for Erin Olson* were lost inside the bent corners and crummy artwork. Now she really felt terrible. Worse than when she started. She glanced down at the paper. Her attempt at comedy had bombed. The speech didn't work. She had made a terrible mistake. She wanted to be funny and entertaining like on television. But she had been wrong. They weren't laughing at all. Not even a little. She pushed the tattered piece of paper back in her pocket.

"Hee, hee," she said with a forced laugh. "I see you didn't like my clowning around. Well, that's good, because I have something important to say. I really want to be your president. I want to work with all the students to make us the best fifth-grade class Mrs. Brambles has ever had."

Wild thoughts ran through her head, and she ignored most of them—except one. She hesitated at first, but after seeing the looks in the audience, she decided to continue. "I want to tell you something about my opponent. Billy Perez is a sneak. He can't be trusted. He attacked me last night in the cemetery and tied me up. He wants to scare me, but I won't be frightened away from this campaign. I am here to prove I can be a good leader."

The students broke out into uncontrollable chatter. Mrs. Brambles clapped her hands, trying to control the storm of upheaval in the room. Everyone became silent. Then everyone turned and looked at Billy.

He jumped up, and pointed a finger at Erin. "She's lying, Mrs. Brambles. I never attacked her. I don't even know what she's talking about. She's just trying to turn everyone against me. She's cheating and should be kicked out of the campaign."

The students looked back and forth from Erin to Billy. The principal whispered something into the teacher's ear and left.

Mrs. Brambles approached the front of the room and placed a hand on Erin's shoulder. "Now let's think about this. Do you have proof of this, dear? This is a very serious charge you have made. Somehow, I find it very hard to imagine that Billy would do such a thing. What would he have to gain?"

Erin looked down, embarrassed. "No, I don't have proof. He ran off before my friend and I could catch him. But I know it's him."

"What happened?" the teacher asked in a soothing voice.

Erin felt her cheeks starting to turn red. Brushing the toe of her shoe across the floor, she began to tell her story. "I found a dead rat on my doorstep yesterday."

The children drew back in their chairs, making icky sounds.

"There was a note tied to the neck and it told me to meet a mystery person under the old maple tree in the cemetery. You know the really old one on the far side. The note said, if I didn't, he would poison the ducks at the pond."

"Oh, my," said Mrs. Brambles, a little alarmed.

"Well, I went to the cemetery and waited, just like the note said. But a boy attacked me from behind. He put a bag over my head and taped my hands behind my back. I couldn't see who it was, but I know it was Billy because he wants to scare me away from being president. And this only happened after we were picked yesterday."

Erin glanced at the back of the room. Billy was grinning.

"Were you hurt?" asked the teacher.

"Not really," she answered sheepishly.

"Why didn't you go to the police, dear?" exclaimed the teacher. "This is exactly what they're for."

Erin shrugged her shoulders and looked down. "Because I wasn't sure who it was. And if it was Billy, I wanted to catch him. Then everyone would know what kind of person he is. "

"But dear, you have already admitted you don't know who attacked you, and then you accused Billy in front of the entire class, without proof. As a candidate running for such an important position, do you think that was wise? Is that the kind of thing a leader does?"

No, thought Erin to herself, not at all. It was the dumbest thing she could have done. Why did she do it? What made her blurt out such a stupid thing? What else was he going to say? Of course he had to deny it. And now she looked like a crybaby and not much of a leader. A good leader, her grandfather had said, gathers all the facts before taking action. Today, she had not shown them what kind of leader she would be.

"I'm sorry, Billy," she announced bravely, "I shouldn't have said anything until I had proof."

"I accept your apology and vow to find the person behind the attack," he boldly replied.

Erin sighed before putting her head down again. She couldn't miss the words coming out of Billy's mouth. He went on to give the best speech she had ever heard, promising to be the best leader around: fair and considerate of others, a person who could solve problems, and a friend. He planned on another computer for the classroom and wanted the elderly people to help in the classrooms. He wanted to campaign for real homemade food in the cafeteria and to start a class honor roll. And last but not least, he announced to everyone that he cared about each and every person, as he personally handed out Tootsie Pops to every student. He placed a chocolate next to Erin.

FIVE

THE BOX

Erin pushed harder and harder, her arms pumping back and forth like an Olympic athlete. It had been five minutes since she left the school, and she was only halfway home. The pennies inside her shoe tops sparkled against the bright afternoon sun. The heels of the black penny loafers clanked against the pavement in a rapid clickety-clack sound. She needed to concentrate. A little faster, she told herself. It wouldn't take much to break the nine-minute record from the school to her house.

The heavy backpack bounced up and down. Her cat, Teddy, was home waiting, and she wanted to tell him about her day: her awful poster, the speech that was the joke of the school, and poor Charlotte Pillman and the horrible woman in the car. And she would be sure to mention the Tootsie Pops. The Tootsie Pops that started the whole school talking and following Billy Perez around like he was a superstar. Teddy wouldn't understand, but she would tell him everything, anyway. And he wouldn't care, but he would look lovingly at her with his large golden eyes and purr. And that's what she needed right now. Closing her eyes, she willed the pennies to go faster.

After rounding the corner to the house, she jumped for joy. According to her watch, she had beaten the old record by twenty seconds. And that was amazing, with her backpack full of heavy psychology and public relations books from the library. The books had stacked like a small mountain. Of course she wouldn't understand everything in them, but she wanted to see them anyway. Passing out Tootsie Pops had been a brilliant move by her very clever opponent. Somewhere in her backpack had to be an idea just as good, if not better.

A familiar sight greeted her on the porch. Temple leaned lazily against the porch swing, his large feet dragging back and forth against the floorboards as he read the newspaper. She tiptoed carefully up the front steps, trying to avoid all the squeaky spots. If she were careful he wouldn't see her.

Temple read the passage in a silly voice. "At Crazy Larry's, we will give you not fifty dollars off, but one hundred dollars off, because folks, we are crazy! Come shop at Crazy Larry's, the place where crazy people shop!"

She slid the heavy backpack from her shoulders and quietly propped the bag against the railing. Squatting down below the edge of the paper was the best place to hide. She waited for the right moment. The swing glided back to the railing before swooping down again. Just as it came within her grasp, she yanked the newspaper down from in front of Temple's face, and yelled, "Ah hah!"

She waited for her favorite expression—the one where his eyebrows shot straight up in surprise. But instead, he grinned, his dark eyes flashing underneath the wire frames.

"You do that every time. You are so predictable. I was only pretending to read the paper. Besides, I could hear you coming. You sounded like a heard of elephants grunting all the way down the street!"

"You're no fun," she mumbled. "And that's not true. I am not predictable."

"Oh, yes, you are," he repeated with a grin. "But still lovable. By the way, I hear 'Bernard-the-weasel' likes you. It seems he has been collecting all the broken pencils you throw into the trash can."

Erin looked helplessly at her friend. Bernard-the-weasel was a strange kid who stared at the girls with his mouth open. She had noticed him staring at her a lot lately. Each fifth-grader had created a game for the Math Fair. All the other kids had long lines waiting to play their games, but Bernard-the-weasel sat all alone against the back wall with his untouched game. No one went near him. Everyone in the fifth-grade had worked hours on his or her project, including him. She only played his game because she didn't want him to feel left out. That was all. And now, he followed her wherever she went.

"Don't worry, Rin, I told him you were my girlfriend and to forget it," Temple said with a puffed out chest.

"And he believed you? That is just great! Everyone at school knows we've been best friends since preschool. I wish you'd stop telling the boys you're my boyfriend. It's not funny anymore. One of these days you're going to chase away my real boyfriend, and I'll never forgive you," she puffed.

"And your point is?" he asked sarcastically.

That was when she spotted the strange package on the floor of the porch, underneath the mailbox. She started for the box.

"How did the poster and speech go?" he asked.

"Don't ask," she replied, and stooped down to take a closer look. "It has been the worst day of my life."

"You mean worse than when Charlotte announced to the whole school who you liked?"

"Worse," she said.

"I bet it was your poster," he quipped. "It stunk. Not your best, My Lady. The message was primitive, and if I were Mrs. Brambles, I would have given you a *D*—for *thoroughly disappointing*."

Erin picked up the backpack, lifted the box off the porch and opened the door. "I know. I'm not going to argue with you today. I underestimated my opponent. You should have seen his poster. Even I wanted to vote for him."

"Really? It was that good? Well, you know Billy's father is a printer and owns his own shop. I've seen posters made by his shop all over town." After folding the newspaper and tucking it under his arm, Temple followed her through the door.

"I didn't know that," she said after throwing her backpack on the couch. "If I'd known that, I would have stayed home last night and polished my poster. He shouldn't be allowed to have outside help. That's cheating."

"Are there rules saying no outside help? You would probably do the same thing if your father was a printer, wouldn't you?" he asked in a smirkish tone.

She glared at him. Temple could be really annoying at times, especially when he was right. Mrs. Brambles hadn't said anything about outside help. It just never had occurred to her to ask anyone for help. She assumed they were personally responsible for everything. Including posters.

"It's still cheating," she protested. "I don't have enough money to buy a poster like that. I had to make mine by hand. And then he brought in a huge bag of Tootsie Pops and passed them out after his speech. That must have cost him two week's allowance."

"I believe . . . " Temple hesitated as he opened the refrigerator door, "That is what all the real candidates complain about. The person with the most money has an unfair advantage. That's why my grandmother never ran for political office. She had the brains and the know-how, but never the money. If you don't have money, nobody listens."

Erin sighed, and turned the address label on the box toward her. "Hey, this is a package for me . . . but there's no postage on it. Someone must have dropped it off. Did you see anyone while you were here?"

"Just a squirrel chasing Teddy down the street," he replied with a chuckle before gulping down a large glass of orange juice. "And that squirrel was really upset. It was nipping at Teddy's feet and clicking at him like mad. I don't think Teddy has the hang of hunting yet. The cat is supposed to chase the squirrel." He wiped his sleeve across the orange-juice mustache.

Erin pulled the box closer.

"Hey, Rin," Temple said in a whisper, "You'd better be careful. That package might explode."

She pushed back from the table in alarm.

Temple laughed. "I was just kidding."

She glowered at her best friend. He could make anyone nervous, with his uncanny way of complicating things. It was just a package and probably nothing more. He just wanted to see her jump. "Who would send me a package?" she muttered, suspiciously turning it with a finger.

"Beats me." Temple removed a brick of cheese from the refrigerator.

"Why would somebody send me a package? It's too soon for my birthday. And the address label on the outside says 'Erin Olson' at this address, but there's no return address and no postmark. There's no way to tell where it's from."

Temple opened the cupboard door and removed the crackers. He lifted a clean plate and a knife from the dishwasher and expertly worked between the crackers and cheese until the plate was full of his favorite snack. "Just go ahead and open it," he said with a mouth full of food.

"What's the big deal? It has your name on it."

"Because too many weird things have been happening. This may be another trick from Billy."

"And maybe it's just a regular everyday package. I wouldn't have mentioned the bomb if I knew you'd take me so seriously. If I really thought there was a bomb in it, would I be sitting here munching on this delicious grub? Think about it, Rin. Billy Perez really does have you rattled."

Erin twitched at the mention of being scared of Billy. "I suppose you're right," she sighed. "But then you're always right." She lifted the package to her ear. "And I don't hear anything ticking. This has to be from the mystery person."

Temple watched as he removed a handful of chocolate chip cookies from the tin on the kitchen counter and sat down. Erin's grandfather had learned to bake since retiring and felt insulted if all the goodies weren't eaten. Temple was obliged to eat as many cookies as he could.

"What's the name of your hospital? It's a good thing to know in case of an emergency," he said before dunking the end of his cookie into a cold glass of milk.

"That's not funny," she snapped. "I find a dead rat on my doorstep, I'm attacked in the cemetery, and I dream about a monster pushing me down all night. Then I humiliate myself at school. Now I come across an unmarked package with my name on it, and you're making jokes about a bomb."

"I repeat, your point is?" he asked after biting off a large chocolate chip from the milk-soaked edge.

"Something strange is going on." She crossed her arms like a schoolteacher. "Billy Perez said he wasn't in the cemetery."

"What!" Temple choked on a mouthful of food. "You confronted him without me? I thought we agreed not to do that." He quickly poured himself another glass of milk and drank it down. He looked directly into Erin's eyes. "Now Billy knows we're on to him. You've just made our job impossible."

"Maybe." She rested her head on the table. "I was stupid, but I couldn't help myself. The words flew out of my mouth before I could stop them. Even I couldn't believe what I was saying. Do you think other presidential candidates have that problem? Of course, Billy denied it."

Temple looked troubled. He turned away deep in thought. The room was silent. Erin stared at the fallen chocolate chips on the tabletop, knowing her trusted friend would smile at any moment. Temple would know how to fix things, and then he would laugh at her and tell her everything would work out. He always did.

"Well . . . the harm is already done," he said mischievously. "We'll just have to deal with things as they happen. Now, let's open the box and see what's in there."

Erin pushed the box out into the middle of the table. As amateur snoops, they had studied every mysterious footprint, every crack, every inch of the dark attic and every object unearthed in the garden. They never found anything very interesting, but they always knew the day would come . . .

They decided the plain brown wrapping paper on the outside of the box could be purchased anywhere. The tan cord tied twice around the outside and crossing as an "X" on the bottom was available at the corner drugstore. They didn't hear anything when Temple rocked the package back and forth. Erin could lift the box from the table with one hand.

"Not very heavy," she said, and then she slid it across to her friend.

Temple balanced it on his outstretched palm. He agreed.

Pulling a pair of scissors from the kitchen drawer, Erin snipped the tan cord. It sprung open, leaving the brown wrapper still intact. Temple pulled out his pocketknife and sliced the cellophane tape sealing the paper seams. The wrapper fell away in waves. Underneath all the wrapping stood a plain white box.

Erin looked anxiously at her friend. "There are no markings on the outside. We have to lift the lid."

"No markings at all?" he asked.

"Not a one," she said.

"Okay, but be really careful," he said cautiously.

She bit her lower lip and reached for the white lid. It wasn't fastened. She pried the corner up and waited. Nothing happened. There weren't any noises—no escaping steam, no loud boom, nothing unusual at all. Temple nodded and she pulled the entire top up. They both stood so they could see. Inside the cardboard walls was another container snug against the sides. It was a wooden crate the size of a shoebox.

Temple slipped his fingers around the newly discovered crate and lifted it up. He placed it on the table in front of them. A round circle of red wax, the size of a fifty-cent piece, sealed each side of the crate. Erin ran her fingers over the hard wax surface.

"What is that stuff?" Temple asked.

"It's sealing wax, and I feel ridges in it," she said, running her fingers back and forth. She knew about imprinting hidden impressions. Last summer, she had visited a historical gravesite with her family. Time had worn down the carved words on the front of the stone markers so they were impossible to read. Her grandfather, however, had showed her how to place a piece of paper over the weathered letters and rub gently with the side of a pencil. With each rub of the pencil, they had discovered word after word on the unreadable surface. Every word had shown up, just like when the marker was new.

"These seals are like the ones used in medieval days," she explained with excitement. "We studied about them in fourth grade. If you were nobility, you had your own special coat of arms made into a seal. You would melt wax onto a surface, and then press the seal into the middle while it was still warm. When it dried, the seal appeared permanently in the wax. If we rub the outside surface with paper and pencil, we'll be able to find something."

"Now you're really going too far, My Lady," Temple said with an amused note. "Do you really think someone went to all that trouble? That is just lumpy wax. Some dope leaned it against a bumpy surface when it was still warm, that's all." He bent down for a better look.

"Temple, we have to check every possibility. You know that's the first rule of good detective work. We don't know who is behind these things or why."

She pulled out paper, laid it across the wax, and rubbed the side of her pencil across the surface. The emerging lines appeared as random marks until the faint outline of a letter appeared. Temple's gaze didn't stray, as he blindly opened the cookie tin and removed another cookie. Erin gripped the small end of the lead and rubbed it nimbly around the edges.

"Hmm . . . " grunted Temple. "You are going to make a good president. There was something mysterious inside the wax. That looks like the letter 'E.'"

Erin repeated her rubbing on each side of the crate, labeled each page, and then placed all four sheets neatly in a row. Temple hovered above, chewing loudly. A chocolate chip dropped on top of the first rubbing.

"Temple, please don't eat around the clues," Erin huffed. She flicked the chip from the paper.

"Sorry, Rinny," he said, apologetically. The rest of the cookie disappeared into his mouth.

"Now," she continued, her finger pointing to the middle of the page, "I think that is definitely a 'B.' 'B' as in 'Billy.' It looks like he touched the wax while it was warm to distort the shape. He was trying to cover up the 'B.' He didn't count on us discovering his trick."

Temple's face was screwed up in disbelief. "Are you sure that's not an 'E'? Maybe it was 'E' for 'Erin.' You can't really tell if those are wavy 'B's' or crooked 'E's'."

"No," stated Erin proudly. "I'm sure those are 'B's.' 'B' for 'Billy.'"

"I will agree that it might be a 'B', but I want to go on record as saying I think it is an 'E' for Erin." He continued to examine each paper under the light. "Okay, what do we do now?"

"We open the crate," she said quietly.

SIX

Rocky as a Mountain

The sealing wax popped when Erin pulled the lid loose from the crate. A shower of hard red wax crumbled to the floor below. Pieces of wood had splintered underneath her hand. She released her grip and cautiously stepped back.

"I want to be the one who looks inside," demanded Temple. "You're having all the fun."

She shook her head no and concentrated on the splinters lodged in her hand. She ignored Temple's grumbling. Since the package had been addressed to her, she wanted to look inside first—especially if it turned out to be dangerous. Temple was an innocent bystander, and besides, she too was anxious to see what was inside.

Temple reached across the table and grabbed hold of the crate. Startled, Erin dug her nails into the back of his hands. Knowing that was something he hated, she wasn't surprised to hear him squeal. He lunged at the crate and pushed her aside.

"Stop it, Temple!" She tugged the crate in the opposite direction. "You'd look hideous with only half a face."

Pulling his hand back to rub the red gashes, he answered mockingly, "Poor Rinny, risking her life to protect me . . . going down with the ship like a sea captain. I'm soooo touched." He placed an opened hand across his heart and pretended to swoon.

Erin rolled her eyes. Temple laughed hysterically. They looked down at the top together. It had been ripped off in all the commotion, and inside the crate was another box. Erin laughed because there hadn't been anything to worry about. It was just a plain, ordinary box. She and Temple stared at it.

"This person is very clever," he said, pointing to his brain. "These must be Chinese boxes, where each box has a smaller box inside. Why would somebody do this?"

Erin lifted the next lid. There was, indeed, a smaller box, with an even smaller box inside that. She uncovered two more boxes before finally coming to the last one. This one was so tiny it looked like it had been a jewelry box. She set it on top of her outstretched hand, the lid still intact.

"Do you think someone sent me a ring?" she asked suspiciously.

"I bet it's from Bernard-the-weasel," Temple said dreamily.

She smiled to herself. Temple behaved strangely every time a boy wanted to be her friend, and she wasn't sure why. He could never be replaced. As her best friend, he had always been there. It was his face she saw after falling off the jungle gym and breaking her arm. And it was Temple who found Tang, her goldfish, dead on the floor. Poor Tang had jumped out of the goldfish bowl, only to have his slimy carcass stepped on by Temple in his bare feet. And it was Temple she trusted with all her secrets. Even when she was grown and married, Temple would still be her friend.

She removed the lid from the smallest box.

"Just what I thought," Temple huffed. "There isn't anything inside. Someone is testing you.'

Erin turned the smallest box over in her hand. "What do you mean by 'test?'"

"I don't know exactly how," he replied, "but there's a reason someone put this package together, then delivered it to your doorstep. The question is why?"

Erin stared at the center of her hand. The tiny box had been the heart of all the other boxes. Everything had led to the middle, but why? There were no marks on the outside, and it, too, was just another ordinary box that could be found anywhere. What did it all mean, she wondered?

"Why would Billy do this?" she asked, picking up the first box again. "What does this have to do with the campaign, unless it's to embarrass me? He thinks I'm going to accuse him in front of the class again. I don't think so. What would I accuse him of? Of giving me an empty box? The class would laugh. He can play all the silly tricks he likes. I won't say a word." She pinched her lips together.

Temple looked at her sympathetically. "You are absolutely right, my dear. Whining isn't very presidential. People don't want leaders who complain. They want leaders who make things happen. Accusing Billy of sending you an empty box wouldn't be smart at all."

Maybe the boxes themselves were a clue, Erin thought. It would have been good to have the fingerprint set featured in the front window of the science store. The one she had wanted for Christmas. But Grandfather had told her to choose between the spy kit and the authentic magician set, and when she did her one potato, two potato, three potato more, the spy kit lost. Unfortunately, pulling quarters out of people's ears didn't help now.

She started with the largest box and, after carefully examining each one, turned them upside-down and stacked them according to size. She decided the boxes were just plain cardboard containers, except for the crate of course, with no hidden flaps or false bottoms and no signs of tampering. Every edge was glued down in its original position. Disheartened, she pushed the boxes away.

The lids lay before her. Deep in thought, she began stacking them one on top the other as she had the boxes, just like a pyramid. Chewing nervously on a fingernail, she gazed at her new creation. Her class had studied the Egyptian pyramids in social studies, learning about hidden chambers and the making of mummies. And Billy had walked around the room with stiff arms and legs, proclaiming to be a mummy sent by King Tutu from the House of PuPu, chanting he had crossed the river Styx in search of bodies. The mummy had pulled Erin stiffly by the ponytail, while Mrs. Brambles chatted with another teacher in the hallway. Erin remembered his face when Mrs. Brambles came in and told the mummy he would be responsible for scrubbing every single desk in the classroom.

Temple watched her. "It's just a stack of lids," he muttered.

"Don't be so impatient. I'm thinking," she said calmly. "There's a clue; I can feel it."

The room was silent as she circled the table twice, viewing the stack of lids from every direction before returning to the side. She reached out and picked up the smallest lid. "Look at this," she whispered with enthusiasm.

Her finger pointed to the inside of the tiny lid. Black scratches completely covered the inside of the top. Excitement grew in her voice. "I wouldn't normally look inside a lid, but when I thought about all the possibilities, I realized people don't expect anything of a lid. They put it off to the side, like I did. I checked all the bottoms but not the tops. I automatically assumed a clue would be sitting inside. That was my mistake."

"Clever girl," Temple mused.

"These scratches look like words. Almost too small to read," she said studying the lid with difficulty. "Only a fine-tipped craft pen would have a point this small. My mother uses one for writing little teeny tiny words on her art projects. Do you have a magnifying glass?"

Temple snorted before reaching deep into his pockets, and pulling out the two white linings. He patted the front of his button-down pockets to demonstrate they were empty. He pulled up the cuffs of his trousers and searched the rims of his socks. Then he pulled off one shoe at a time and sniffed before looking inside. He eyed Erin with a crooked smirk. Then he walked two fingers across the tabletop like legs and pretended to sniff her empty pockets. Placing a finger against his chin, he stated, "That no-good-sneaky magnifying glass has run off again. Sorry."

Erin couldn't help but laugh out loud.

After straightening himself up, he spoke in a more serious manner. "Well, what does the lid say?"

She strained with furrowed brow to see inside the tiny top. She stopped and glared at Temple. His head was blocking the sunlight coming in from the kitchen window. The words were really hard to read, and she needed every ray of sun. In fact, the writing was so tiny, she couldn't tell if they were letters or ink smudges. She thought of stomping on his toes, knowing he would have to jump out of the way. But she resisted. Sherlock Holmes never scolded Dr. Watson for his participation, and neither would she.

She knew the anonymous author had struggled to write in such a small space. She imagined a stream of perspiration dripping from the tip of Billy's nose as he struggled to form each miniature letter. Hovering above his shoulder would be a bright spotlight. He would have held the pen in one hand, and a magnifying glass in the other. She sighed. Billy Perez had brains *and* patience to manage such a difficult task.

After a long silence, she began to whisper under her breath.

Temple waited impatiently. "I can't hear you."

She smiled at last. The teeny tiny words had come together as a message. At first the words didn't make any sense, but now she understood. The little box top had been the next clue, and she had almost missed it. The packaging and empty boxes were only a distraction. They were part of the game. Obstacles. Something to take your eyes off the goal.

Beaming with pride, she recited the verse from memory.

> *"What is rocky as a mountain,*
> *Lower than a lake,*
> *Three ways to go,*
> *Nineteenth-century date."*

Then she stared off into space, totally clueless as to what that meant.

SEVEN

THE SKI MASK

Temple leaned against the shiny chrome frame of the 1950s kitchen chair. The dinette set with the turquoise Formica top had been moved into the kitchen three years ago with the arrival of Erin's grandfather. Matching turquoise curtains hung above the windows. The chairs' vinyl seat covers were famous for sticking to bare flesh. Everyone wearing shorts or a bathing suit and sitting on these chairs in the hot summer months found themselves glued to the vinyl like masking tape.

Dressed in long jeans, Erin knew her legs were safe from the skin-sucking vinyl monster. She helped herself to the remaining cookie left in Grandfather's tin. Temple had refused to help her decipher the meaning to the riddle, so she wrote it down. Grandfather always said if she placed things in front of her, maybe the brain could put it all together.

"I love riddles," exclaimed Temple as he balanced his weight on the back legs of his chair. "And this is a really good a riddle. *What is rocky as a mountain?* Hmm . . . I wonder what that means. . . *Lower than a lake,* hmm . . .that's a hard one . . . *Three ways to go* . . . now that's a stumper . . . and then finally, *Nineteenth-century date.* What does it all mean?"

Before Erin could say anything, he fell over backwards in the chair. He jumped up acting like nothing had happened and brushed his clothes off. His head twitched as he stood the chair upright.

Erin grinned. Temple falling over in his chair wasn't anything new. The fact that he was never hurt was the amazing thing. And she didn't understand why he kept leaning back so far. He knew if you lean back, you fall over. She let out a long sigh. Maybe it wasn't the understanding that mattered. Maybe he just liked leaning back and falling.

"This is an excellent riddle," he started again, as if she hadn't heard him the first time. He teetered backwards. "I especially like the 'three ways to go.' That could be anything: three different streets leading to the same place, three different entrances, three different locations, or three totally different towns." He reached for the small lid sitting across the table. "Just think of the possibilities."

Erin studied the riddle and, pretending the tabletop was a typewriter, drummed away in thought and shushed Temple. "Shhh, I'm trying to think . . . what is rocky as a mountain, but lower than a lake?"

The tap, tap, tap echoed across the kitchen. Chewing on her lower lip, she thought about the presidential race. She couldn't claim to be a leader if she couldn't solve the riddle. A class president had to be smart, decisive and a good team player. And right now, she needed to be a leader by solving the problem.

Temple suddenly jumped up with a loud thud. Erin looked up to see him pinch his lips shut with a finger and thumb.

"You figured out the answer, didn't you?" she asked.

He squeezed his lips even tighter and turned an imaginary key. He pretended to drop the key inside his pocket.

Erin turned away from the comical pose. She didn't dare smile—he would continue. Her reputation as a leader depended on her figuring out the answer. As tempting as it was to ask Temple for the answer, she had to solve this herself!

"'Nineteenth-century date' means the 1800s," she said in a loud, decisive voice. Always before, the word 'century' had confused her. But when Mrs. Brambles taught the class to go back one hundred years, she realized the twentieth-century was referring to things that had happened in the 1900s. The eighteenth century meant the 1700s. And the nineteenth century meant the 1800s. And there were many places in town dating back to the 1800s.

Temple released his pinched lips to bow with approval. "Well done, my dear."

"Okay, so it has to do with the 1800s. But how does that relate to the rest of the riddle?" she asked.

Like a performer enjoying the attention of an audience, Temple motioned high in the air before pinching his lips shut again.

Scowling this time, Erin turned away again. He looked like a cartoon duck with big, fat lips. "What is rocky as a mountain?" she whis-

46

pered to herself. Tuttle Park, where the soccer teams played, was rocky in places, but not like a mountain. And the construction site where they had piled the dirt into a mountain was now gone. In its place stood a shopping mall with green grass and trees. The quarry had been full of rocks at one time but was now full of water. A large sign said, "Stay Out" because of jagged rocks underneath.

"Give me a little hint," she pleaded. "Not the answer, just a tiny little clue."

"No," he said stiffly. "You wouldn't let me look in the box first, so you'll have to figure out the riddle by yourself."

She put her chin on her fists on the table, and stared straight ahead. After a moment she glanced his way. He shook his head no in a very dramatic way. She frowned. Temple Black could figure out anything. Her favorite name for him was Mr. Know-it-all, until he claimed she was being mean and demanded she stop.

"Okay, I'll go to the next line. 'Lower than a lake.' I didn't know anything could be lower than a lake." She got up and paced the floor in thought. "There isn't anything lower than a lake, except . . . except something deep inside the ground!"

Temple let out a small smile.

"Caverns are big holes underground . . . they could be lower than a lake," she said, spinning around. "And a cavern is rocky inside!"

Temple nodded yes, yes, yes, over and over.

She clapped her hands together. "Soooo, the riddle is talking about a cavern of some kind. One that has three ways to go." She paced around the table, stepping over her friend's big feet, trying to fit all the pieces together. Eighteen hundreds, rocky, underground, three ways to go.

She stopped. Temple held his breath waiting for her to speak.

"There's only one answer!" she exclaimed. "The tin mine!"

Temple applauded.

Of course, she thought to herself, it had to be the mine. The tin mine had been dug in the early nineteenth-century. The town had grown up around the mine, because families moved there for the work. Then the mine had closed a hundred years later because mineral prices had started going up and down, becoming unreliable and driving the owners out of business. Thirty years ago, the mine was reopened as a national museum. Now, the public entered the mine to take guided tours underground.

Erin waved three fingers proudly in the air. "And there are three different paths going through the mine: one easy, the second more difficult, and the third so hard, you have to crawl on hands and knees."

Temple jumped for joy. "Well done, Rinny. I knew you would get it. And I just read in the paper that the President of the United States will be campaigning for re-election at the mine tomorrow. Seems he's giving the town money to help with the flood damage caused by last month's storm. Want to go and see him?"

"See him!" cried Erin. "I want to talk to him! Who knows more about campaigning than the President? And I want to talk with him about some of my ideas too."

She would even break out her new Coca-Cola pen, along with the new flip pad featuring the Coca-Cola polar bear on front. And, across the front of her brand new pad, she would write, "MY INTERVIEW WITH THE PRESIDENT OF THE UNITED STATES," in bold letters. She stood proudly at attention, just thinking about it.

But her mood changed quickly. As she turned toward the kitchen window, something made her heart stop. Two eyes were staring at her from behind a ski mask. She blinked and the slinky shape slipped below the windowsill and out of sight.

"Someone was spying on us!" she shrieked. She grabbed hold of Temple's shirt and pushed him toward the door. A quick tug on the door handle opened it. She shoved him through. "Hurry, Temple, catch Billy before he gets away!"

And with the wink of an eye, Temple leapt through the doorway and took off running like the wind.

EIGHT

THE PRESS SECTION

A rooster crowed. Erin opened the front door as the bright morning sun glistened off the dew. On top of the doormat lay the morning newspaper; a large picture of the President covered the front page. Pushing the door all the way open, she picked up the morning paper and let her friend in, who was bounding up the front steps. A broad smile accentuated his large, mischievous eyes. Long, dark eyelashes fluttered under the wire-framed glasses.

"Morning, Rinny. Good day to see the President and visit the mine, don't you think?" Temple said cheerfully.

Erin nodded, before placing the newspaper on the kitchen table. She finished brushing her ponytail, grabbed two bagels, and then unhooked her jacket from the peg. After handing Temple a bagel covered in sesame seeds, she closed the door behind them. Today they were leaving three hours early so they could get to the mine before the crowd. So far, they were right on schedule.

"Are you sure there wasn't anyone near the house last night?" she asked for the third time since the incident with the ski mask. "I know I saw Billy staring at me."

"Honest, Rin, I didn't see him. I ran twice around the entire block. If he was there, he managed to disappear without a trace. And that would be hard to do, because I was smokin'!" He grinned with pride. After thinking silently for a moment, he continued, "Maybe I should mention this . . . It still doesn't seem important, but I thought I saw Bernard-the-weasel in the back alley. When I ran over to see who it was, the person was gone. It was probably someone taking out the trash. And the person I saw wasn't wearing a ski mask and didn't appear to be carrying one."

Erin looked down at the sidewalk. That meant she couldn't believe her own eyes. If her best friend didn't trust her, no one would. And she knew she saw a person wearing a ski mask and looking in the window yesterday afternoon. And Billy Perez has worn such a mask on the playground plenty of times. But then, so did all the boys when the weather was cold, including Bernard-the-weasel. To Erin, the really strange thing was, it wasn't cold enough to wear a ski mask. That meant this person was hiding his or her identity.

Saturday mornings were perfect for watching cartoons and eating pancakes as far as Erin was concerned. But it wasn't every day the President of the United States came to town. Her grandfather had said the President was only coming because he had made the people angry and wanted to make them happy again. That way he could ask for their votes. He was speaking today and presenting a check to the people so they could fix the damage caused by last month's flood. Television crews would be there to broadcast the event nationally. Grandfather said the President wouldn't miss the opportunity to play Santa Claus in front of TV cameras, and Erin didn't really know what he meant by that. What was so bad about helping restore the mine?

Streams of cars passed by. The traffic became heavier as they neared the entrance. Upon arriving, they found cars, vans, trucks and people jammed together in a state of confusion. Surrounding the gridlock were television cameras, reporters, the high school marching band and vendors. A local radio station, housed inside a large van with a picture window, was parked next to the curb. An announcer sporting a hi-tech headset sat perched behind a control board and waved to the people as they passed. A large touring coach blocked the entranceway.

The speech wouldn't take place for hours, but a pushing-room-only crowd was gathered already. Temple fought his way through, pulling Erin directly into gouging elbows and crushing shoulders. A policeman stood at the front and pointed them toward the press section. Men in blue patrolled the grounds. A thick yellow rope supporting a "DO NOT ENTER" sign stretched across the press section. In front of them, stood a stage surrounded by lights mounted on long poles.

Erin pulled the special press passes from her pocket. It had taken her grandfather all night to get them. He had still been on the phone when she went to bed. She pinned a special pass onto the outside of her jacket and the other on Temple. An officer waved both of them through. They pushed their way to the front.

"Children are not allowed in the press section," declared the man in front of them. His beady eyes didn't move. Inside an exposed pocket stood a Mont Blanc pen. A red paisley tie swayed in the wind. His crisp blue sport jacket hung perfectly from his shoulders. He patted the top of his balding head, trying to smooth his wind-tossed hair.

"We're here to interview the President," replied Erin proudly. "We represent Franklin Elementary." She flashed him the press pass, pulled out the new Coca-Cola pen and notebook, and then held the notebook up for him to see. "MY INTERVIEW WITH THE PRESIDENT OF THE UNITED STATES."

The man scoffed. "The President won't talk to you, little girl. If he talks at all, it will be to the entire press corps. Even then he only calls on certain reporters—grown-up reporters. Sometimes his press secretary does the talking. Didn't your school teach you anything? It's the press secretary's job to talk to the reporters and tell them what the President's doing," he snorted. "We ask our questions to her. And you're not even old enough to vote, so I doubt either the President or the press secretary will even look at you."

"But, I'm running for president of my fifth-grade class, and I need to ask the President some important questions about his job," insisted Erin. She flipped to the first page of the spotless notebook.

The man let out a belly laugh. "We all have our reasons. I'm afraid the President is too busy for a mere child. But if you stay out of the way and keep quiet, maybe you'll learn something."

Erin shoved the pen back into her pocket and gazed down at the pebbles surrounding her feet. She hadn't realized you couldn't talk to the President. Then how did the President know what was going on . . . what the problems were . . . what people really need? She only knew what the class needed because she was part of it.

More people poured into the press section. As the crowd pushed them forward, her big toe caught under the boot in front of her. The man leaned back. She grimaced in pain. Then a small figure squeezed past her. She looked up in time to see the person wink. "Billy Perez!" she gasped. "What are you doing here?"

"The same as you. I'm here to interview the President, too," he said, looking across her shoulder at Temple. He watched Temple for a long time. Erin glanced back at her friend, trying to see what was so interesting, but Temple was staring off in a different direction. His eyes were following the uniformed officers moving through the crowd.

She faced the front again. Billy was grinning at her.

The words she had kept pent up inside poured out. "Why did you attack me in the cemetery?"

Billy's grin disappeared.

"I know it was you at the cemetery and I'll catch you. So you should stop right now, before Temple and I . . . "

"Before Temple and you what?" he asked with raised eyebrows. "Beat me up?"

She paused. Of course, Temple was on her side, and she wanted Billy to know it, but she would never threaten to beat someone up. The thought had never occurred to her. "Before Temple and I tell the sheriff," she said humbly.

Billy glanced at the stage and then quickly turned back. "It wasn't me."

His innocent expression and serious blue eyes baffled her. She was tempted to believe him. He looked like someone you could trust with your deepest secrets. Maybe it really wasn't him, she thought. Maybe she had been too quick to judge. Maybe everything had been a coincidence. Maybe she had been totally wrong. Maybe she had been on the wrong track.

Then he winked and the spell was broken. She came to her senses and remembered the character with whom she was dealing. This was Billy Perez, the king of the clowns. This was the boy who rammed a piece of chalk up his nose and danced around Mrs. Brambles' desk complaining that it smelled. This was the boy who kept changing the contents of people's desks. Erin had found her pink sweetheart eraser in Ted's pencil case with the words, "I LOVE TED" written all over it. And how did Billy know she would be at the mine, unless he had been spying on them? Just yesterday, she had caught him drawing a mustache on her campaign poster. Now the "O" had a smiley face with horns on top *and* a mustache. She looked down for a bag of Tootsie Pops, but his hands were empty.

She moved her feet apart. Then, baring all her teeth, she leaned forward and snarled like a wolf. Grandpa claimed it was her scariest face, and that's what she wanted right now. He had to know she meant business. Billy blinked twice before breaking out in laughter.

"We can look inside the mine first," whispered Temple. Ignoring Erin's growls, he looked up at Billy but looked away just as quickly. Something was on his mind. "The President won't be giving his speech for at least two hours."

Erin watched Billy laugh and laugh. She put her hands on her hips, just like Mrs. Brambles did when she meant business. She gave Billy the laser stare, the same laser stare Charlotte Pillman used to bore holes through her. Billy hesitated before doubling over at the waist and laughing even more hysterically. His roaring cackle echoed as she marched away at Temple's side.

NINE

LOCKED

"I think we should search the mine for another clue before the crowd follows," stated Temple.

They moved past the people and toward the building where the mine's entrance was housed. The opening had been dug in a valley. Large hills and a lake occupied the surrounding area. A brown, rectangular building covered the top of the mining shaft. Toward the front were the gift shop and lecture rooms, and large displays of colorful minerals sparkled through the glass windows. Visible on the far wall of the gift shop stood the entrance to the mine. A sign saying LOCKED, covered the yellow door.

When the mine was open for business, tourists were required to watch a safety presentation before entering. The shaft descended deep into the earth, weaving through the rock like an ant farm. Next to the shaft's entrance were large bins full of helmets in all sizes. No one was allowed to enter the mine without a safety helmet. Guards checked each person before allowing tourists to enter. In the twentieth century, electricity had been installed, but guides carried flashlights as part of their normal gear. It was extremely dangerous to be underground if the lights went out.

Once, several hundred tourists had been trapped below. They had crawled through the shaft, one in front of the other, until they reached the top, where a television crew captured their exit.

Today, a sign on the gift shop door said, "The Mine is Temporarily Closed."

"It's locked . . . we can't get in," Erin said, after twisting the knob with both hands.

"Oh, yes we can," Temple responded. He unbuttoned his jacket and pulled out a small compact of burglary tools. Thin metal instruments were arranged in a neat little row inside the case. "Watch. I can open that door in thirty seconds."

Erin didn't know what to say. She could only stare at him. Who was this boy? Her best friend had a burglary set—tools used by real burglars for stealing real things. The Temple she knew was nice, a brain, a prize-winning athlete, and a person who rescued bugs from swimming pools. "Where did you get that?" she asked in hushed tones.

"I found it in the attic, in my grandfather's old trunk. And I've been practicing on the locks at home. I've been carrying it in my pocket hoping to use it sometime. And this sure seems like the perfect time. It's really quite easy once you figure out how the tumblers work. Listen, Rin, we aren't here to steal anything . . . we're here to find the clue and get an interview with the President. We're just giving ourselves a tour outside of normal hours and won't disturb anything, right?"

Erin pulled nervously at her hair. This was really risky. The LOCKED sign blocking the mine door was written in gigantic letters. Whoever put it up meant business. They would have to get through the gift shop door first and then open the mine door. She heard the gift shop door tumblers fall into place. Temple held the door open. She looked inside the dark room.

Letting out a long sigh she admitted to herself that it was the perfect opportunity to explore the mine for another clue. The President wasn't going to be there for two more hours, and they really didn't have anything else to do, except to stand in the middle of some snippy reporters.

"Okay," she said at last. "But if something goes wrong, I'll be in big trouble. Mrs. Brambles will disqualify me from the campaign, and then Billy Perez will be the automatic winner. And that's not mentioning what my mother and father will do, too."

"Stop worrying, Rin. Things will be all right. I know this mine like the back of my hand. Remember, I was a volunteer guide last summer. I've walked through these shafts backwards and forwards. Trust me; I know what I'm doing," he said softly.

Only thin rays of sunlight seeping through the windows lighted the dark room. Erin could barely see her hands in front of her. She scooted along the wooden floors, trying to avoid the obstacles lining the aisle.

"Stay right here, and I'll get two flashlights," Temple said before disappearing.

His shuffling footsteps faded. She tried to follow the sound but could only stare into complete darkness in that direction. For several moments all she could hear was her own short shallow breaths whooshing in and out. A floorboard creaked behind her—from back where they had just walked—back by the unlatched door.

Erin turned slowly, straining to make out the images in the small trickle of sunlight. The darkened images of tables and shelves were barely visible. The front door was ajar. Daylight broke through the cracks. She had been the last one through the door and was certain she had closed it. She didn't move.

A gust of wind brushed against the wind chimes outside on the porch. The tinkling of chimes rattled in the silence. She searched again slowly, combing the darkness from one side to the other. A stronger gust of wind found the chimes, banging them against each other wildly. Her hand jerked against a stack of pencils. They tumbled to the floor and bounced around her feet. She laughed silently to herself as she picked up the pencils. Of course, she thought, the door wasn't pushed all the way closed, and the wind had blown it open.

"Okay, Rinny, I've got them. Let's go," called Temple from the darkness.

She shuffled toward the front door and closed it again. The wind blew against the wooden frame, but this time the clasp held, and the door remained shut. The flashlight's narrow white beam lit the path before her.

TEN

DOWN, DOWN, DOWN

"I can't see the bottom," Erin whispered.

"That's because it's hundreds of feet down," said Temple calmly.

He held Erin's arm as they leaned over the edge of the cavern with their flashlights. Standing at the top of the shaft, they could see how the walls became narrower toward the bottom. They stood at the largest opening underground.

"See how shiny the wall of the cavern is . . . and how smooth? That's where the miners used to pull the buckets up and down the shaft. The buckets rubbed against the surface and eventually wore down the sides until they were smooth."

"And you think that's where we should go? To the bottom of the cavern?" asked Erin.

She pulled back from the ledge. The cavern looked frightening in the dark. Water could be heard dripping off the walls. The lights bouncing off the rock caused little, eerie shadows to dance around the shaft. Temple's face reminded her of a werewolf as the flashlight's beam highlighted the tip of his long pointed nose, his two ghastly eyes and his enormously bushy eyebrows. The rest of his face was covered in dark shadows and disappeared against the rock. His long, curly, windblown hair circled his face like a lion's mane.

"We'll go to the bottom and work our way up. That's my favorite part of the mine. Over a hundred years ago seven men died down there. They were stealing deposits from a hidden seam of minerals and selling them outside the mine for cash. But, they were stealing from a wall that hadn't been shored-up. That's what they call it when they use wooden beams to keep the walls from crashing in. See, the ground from above is very heavy and pushes down with a lot of weight. When you take out the rock and earth and leave a large hole, it eventually crumbles if there's nothing holding it up."

The light from his flashlight cut into the darkness as he pointed to different areas below. "Well, these miners kept chipping away at the wall until it finally collapsed. A large gust of wind rushed through the tunnel and blew all the candles out, water poured in through the broken rock, and the miners were trapped in the dark. Forty-three of them made it out, but the seven who actually caused the collapse didn't. And no one ever found the bones. Every time I'm there, I try to figure out what happened to the bones."

"I don't understand," said Erin, marveling at the flickering images on Temple's face. "How can they lose the bones? After they cleared the tunnel, wouldn't the bones be there?"

"The lake bottom is not far from the mine. And the silt, which is a thick layer of dirt and water covering the bottom of the lake, came through the broken walls and filled in part of the cavern. The damage was so bad; they had to close the mine. It was decades before the mine reopened, and there wasn't any evidence of the men who had died—just some stories passed down by local townspeople."

Erin clung to his arm as they tiptoed down the steep path chiseled out of rock. Only three feet wide, it required walking in single file. They brushed against the wall of solid granite. Only a railing made of rope protected them from falling into the open shaft.

"What do you think happened to the bones?" asked Erin.

She shuffled to keep up, knowing Temple would want to figure out what had happened. And now she understood why he had volunteered at the mine last summer. He was involved in a mystery . . . the mystery of the missing miners.

"I can't say now. I'm still working on it." He glided effortlessly down the path.

Erin gave her flashlight a squeeze. She didn't want to be like the miners a hundred years ago, trying to crawl up a dark tunnel toward safety.

The seeping water trickled down the rock wall. Small pools gathered in shallow pockets around their feet. Erin looked up. The walls of glittering stone now reached high above. The darkness swallowed the stone in a blanket of black. The path descended down, down, down until they reached the bottom. The walk had seemed like miles. Temple stepped out into a large opening. Erin followed.

"Did you hear something?" whispered Erin. "I'm sure something came down behind us."

"Like what?" asked Temple softly.

"Like footsteps . . . no, more like shuffling."

Temple pointed his light toward the descending path. The beam scanned a wall of rock, outlining the shiny surface and narrow path. The thin beam moved down the path until it fell at their feet. "No one's there," he said.

"What was that?" whispered Erin, her flashlight darting in a different direction. "Didn't you hear it?"

Temple searched until his flashlight merged with hers. Both beams lit the granite wall. A dark hole emerged when they moved the light away.

"That, Rinny, is a specially hollowed out area in the rock," replied Temple. "Before electricity, they hollowed out ledges in the rock where they could set candles to light the tunnels. Those holes are all along here."

"Those ledges don't make noise, do they?" squeaked Erin.

"Of course not, Rinny."

"Well, I know I heard something," she insisted. "And I heard something upstairs in the gift shop when you left to get the flashlights."

"Just like the boy with the ski mask? Rinny, your imagination is playing tricks on you. There is no place to hide. This is the bottom. All the paths go up from here. And from here, you can see most of the way up. See, no one is here," he said sweeping the walls with his flashlight again.

"But our flashlights aren't strong enough to light up the entire place. Someone could be moving around and hiding," mumbled Erin.

"The path down is narrow and bumpy. We would be able to see if someone had another flashlight, and only a fool would follow us down without one. Everyone knows you could easily fall over the side without light, and there's no one lying on the ground." Temple swept the light across the bottom again. "See, no dead bodies. Now can we search for the clue?"

"Okay," mumbled Erin again. "But don't be surprised if we bump into someone."

"Now," he said, pointing to the back of the landing, "we should split up. You search one side and I'll search the other. Make sure you check every inch, because these rocks have openings. And you never know what you'll find." Then he walked away.

ELEVEN

Something Strange

Erin spotted a small opening between the smooth, speckled surfaces of two gigantic boulders. The monstrous rocks stacked like a solid wall of giant building blocks, the edges fitting snugly together like pieces of a jigsaw puzzle. The gap at the base was just wide enough for a hand.

"Temple," she called out. "Are there any rats or snakes down here?"

"There weren't any before the flood," he yelled back. "But the water was a hundred feet high down here. It washed out many of the large rocks that hadn't been disturbed for centuries. Who knows what's crawling around now. That's one of the reasons the mine has been closed. The rocks need to be anchored before it opens again."

"Now he tells me," she mumbled to herself. It was just like him not to mention they were going into an area, hundreds of feet below the surface, with unstable rocks the size of cars . . . large, heavy rocks teetering on the edge . . . rocks that could flatten a person like a pancake. Big flat human pancakes, with eyes, ears and little squashed noses. And they would lie there for eternity because the mine was closed.

She considered the opening again. The triangular shaped crevice was underneath a wide ledge. But if she placed the flashlight on the ground, and pointed it toward the hole, she would have both hands free to explore. And if she laid flat on her stomach, she'd be able to scoot underneath the ledge and reach deeper inside.

The flashlight's beam lit the interior of the small hole. Erin rolled up her sleeves and crawled underneath the rock's edge until she reached the opening. A small trickle of water seeped through the crack above and dripped onto her cheek. She viewed the inside of the illuminated rock. A small puddle of water reflected the light.

The coolness of the air and the temperature of the water made her fingers feel icy cold. It was a long reach into the back of the crevice. Goose bumps tingled across her skin. The wet, rough surface turned to mud and pebbles. Finally, she touched the back wall, feeling a small ledge jutting out from the rock. Her frigid fingers combed the edge. Wide on one end, the ledge suddenly dropped off. Wedged against the wall underneath was an object the size of a grapefruit.

Erin tugged at the round object until it rolled toward her. She cupped it in her hand. It was not round like a ball, but lumpy and oddly shaped—a smooth surface on one side and rough on the other. Realizing the crevice opening wasn't wide enough for both her hand and the object to pass through, she frowned. This was a hand-in-the-cookie-jar dilemma. She could pull her hand out empty but not with the object in it.

"Rin! Come here! I found something," shouted Temple, anxiously.

"Just a minute . . . " she answered, trying to free her arm.

"Rin, hurry! I want you to see this!" he repeated anxiously again.

Her hand was stuck. She had squeezed her hand around the object and moved it close enough to the opening that now she couldn't pull her hand away. She twitched frantically back and forth, the movement only making matters worse. A sharp pain shot across her knuckles. Her fingers were trapped between the wall and the object she was holding. Her hand was throbbing, and she couldn't let go. She couldn't even stretch out her fingers.

"Rinny, hurry!"

She closed her eyes. Think, she told herself. Stay calm . . . think it through. What was she supposed to do? Temple wouldn't be able to lift the boulder away, and they couldn't send for help. They had broken into a restricted area—a restricted area expecting the President of the United States and filled with undercover agents. And what would be her excuse when the fire department came? That she lost a hair barrette under this large rock? She moaned just thinking about the trouble she'd be in. Then the answer suddenly came to her. The object needed to be pushed back into the widest part of the gap so she would have enough room to open her fingers. Then she could let go.

She pushed against the rock as hard as she could, willing her aching arm to reach just a little further. The muscles screamed in pain as her knuckles scraped against the jagged wall. She grunted, reaching further and further. By flipping over on her side, she gained another inch. It worked. She was finally able to push the object free with her thumb.

She wiggled free of the ledge.

"Hurry up! It *is* your clue," he said impatiently.

"I hear you, Temple," she snapped back. Holding her hand under the light, she massaged her swollen and bruised knuckles. Temple could wait. The clue could wait. Everything could wait. There was something mysterious inside this hole and she wanted to know what it was. The question was how to get it out.

"Do you have any string?" she asked.

"Nope," he said walking toward her. The light from his flashlight threw off a ghastly shadow against the boulders. "But, your clue has a chain on it."

Erin sat up. Temple knelt down and shined the flashlight on what was in his hand. A golden locket sparkled under the bright light.

"Why didn't you come?" he demanded. The flickering shadow of his curly hair danced across the rock like wriggling snakes. "I wanted to show you where I found it. The chain was hanging out from a small crack in the rock."

"I was stuck," she said, lifting the locket from his hand. "There is something weird behind that rock, and I want to see it, but the opening is too small for me to pull it out with my hand. I thought maybe I could slip a string around it and pull it through."

Before examining the locket, she showed him her bloody hand under the light. He mumbled words of sympathy. Satisfied that he understood the problem, she held the locket up to the light. She squinted when she saw it. It looked really familiar. But it couldn't be, she thought. How could it be in the mine? There could only be one oval locket with a rose gold etching on the front. She looked at the chain and then at Temple.

"This is *my* locket . . . my father gave this to me when I was five. See . . . the chain . . . I broke it when I was wrestling with my cousin. I keep it in my jewelry box. How did it get here?"

Temple shrugged. "Beats me? Maybe there are two of them."

"But the chain snapped just like this one! It didn't break in the middle; it broke near the clasp, leaving one end very short and one really long. We never replaced it . . . and the inside will be empty because I never put a picture in it."

Temple leaned forward with his flashlight. They stared at the front of the locket. Trickling water sounded in the distance. Distorted shapes danced along the walls.

Temple gave Erin an excited look and nodded. She slowly pried the top up, trying to keep her hand still. The opened locket rocked back and forth in her swollen hand. They both leaned into the light for a better look.

Erin gasped first. "This is a photograph of Miss Haggerty, the old maid who lives in the haunted mansion! Why would there be a photograph of *her* in *my* locket?"

Under the bright glow of light, Temple's werewolf eyes focused on the picture. The wriggling snakes of hair moved across the rocks. "Maybe it's *her* locket," he murmured.

"But, it's *my* locket. See, the back says, *Love Dad*. Someone broke into my jewelry box, stole my locket and placed a picture of Miss Haggerty inside. Then he hid it inside the mine so we would find it. But why?"

"I don't know, but I know this . . . this person is clever . . . clever like a fox." His worried expression showed in the creepy lighting.

Erin sat silently, turning the locket over and over again. Temple tried to take the locket from her fingers, but she suddenly squeezed her hand shut.

"I've got it!" she said. "The person wearing the ski mask broke into my bedroom. I saw him as he was leaving. No wonder he disappeared so quickly . . . he had an escape route already planned out. And who shows up today? None other than Billy Perez! He arrives at the mine early and plants the locket. Then we bump into each other in the press section. I ask him what's he doing here, and he says he's here to interview the President—*just like me*. See, that proves he overheard us talking in the kitchen. I told you Billy was looking in the window. The sneak had just stolen the locket from my jewelry box."

"But . . . I didn't see Billy when I looked outside. I still think it's a different locket . . . a lot of lockets say, *Love Dad*. The whole thing is probably a coincidence." Behind Temple's head, danced the ghostly snakes. They jerked wildly across the rock as the flashlights moved about.

Erin studied the look on Temple's face and then sat deep in thought. She finally spoke. "Well, we'll just have to ask Miss Haggerty," she said. "She's the only one who can answer our questions now. But first, I want to see what's in this hole."

"Yes, ma'am," said Temple with a military salute. A long, spindly shadow imitated the gesture against the wall. "Wise decision, My Lady." Then he moved closer to the opening in the rock. "Hey, maybe you found one of the miners' bones."

"The chain can't be used as a piece of string," Erin said, after pulling the Coca-Cola pen from her pocket. "It's not long enough. But I have another idea."

She crawled back under the rock and reached into the opening, this time with her Coca-Cola pen between her fingers. She found the round object. After placing the pen directly behind the base of the object, she edged it toward her. It started to move forward, then stopped. The passageway had become too narrow for both her wrist and the object.

She set the pen down on the cold surface and felt the outside of the object. There were two interesting dents. She pushed against one of them with her thumb, feeling the small hole inside. It was soft and spongy, a texture the pen might be able to grasp. She pushed the pen inside the hole and pulled. It stayed intact.

Wiggling the object at an angle, she dragged it toward the opening. It became a struggle to clear the gap. She squirmed back and forth trying to get just the right slant so she could clear the opening with her hand. It was tricky trying to maneuver the object with the pen. A jerk of her foot accidentally sent the flashlight rolling away. The area blackened as the object cleared the space. Temple pointed his light at the opening and gasped. Erin grabbed her flashlight and sat up, shining the beam directly at her new discovery. She yanked her hand away. The Coca-Cola pen dropped to the floor.

"It's a cat's head, Rinny!" exclaimed Temple. "A decomposing cat's head!"

Erin scooted away on her bottom, trying to get away from her find.

"Aw . . . the skin's missing from the back of the skull, but look," he said in a startled voice, "there's fur still attached to the face. Poor little thing . . . there's an ear, a nose and teeth. All its teeth are still there. It was a calico cat. Look at the different colors of the fur." He rotated the head under the light.

Erin shook her head back and forth.

"The poor thing must have drowned in the flood," Temple said quietly. "And the flood waters carried it down here and washed it under the rocks . . . and Rinny! Look! Here's the hole you made. You stuck your pen in the cat's eye!"

He stared at her with a long face.

She settled against the rock wall, crossing her legs Indian style. With her head cocked to one side, she began wiping her hands across the legs of her jeans, over and over again. No one spoke a word. Temple placed the head gently on the ground.

"Rinny, are you all right?" he asked.

After a long silence, she lifted her head and, finding the pen on the ground, wiped it clean across the sleeve of her shirt. Staring through her friend as if he were a ghost, she clicked the pen open and shut several times before slipping it blindly into her pocket. Then, flashlight in hand, she walked away.

TWELVE
THE WOMAN WITH THE PENCIL-DRAWN EYEBROWS

The bright morning sun was blinding after the darkness of the mine. The cool autumn wind blew effortlessly across the ground. Small gusts of leaves twirled and danced along with the breeze before suddenly crashing to the ground. A loud hum filled the air. The talkative crowd grew larger as rumors of the President's arrival spread. Erin felt like her head was swimming from all the commotion.

Pushing through the crowd of reporters, she made her way to the front row, where the stage overlooked the press section. Making it through the crowd hadn't been easy. The reporters were knocking each other over for the best positions, and she had to shove and elbow her way through—even pinch the enormous man blocking her view.

The President was going to speak any minute, and the people were restless. She ran her fingers through her knotted hair. The tangles were stubborn against the effort. She didn't need a mirror to tell her she was an absolute mess. And who wouldn't be after exploring a wet, dirty cavern? Her clothes were filthy from crawling around on the ground, and the knees of her pink jeans were so muddy they looked like two brown patches.

Before entering the crowd, she had stopped and rinsed her hands and the pen with bottled water—bottled water costing $3.00. It had cost her an entire week's allowance, but the $3.00 had been worth it. At least her hands were clean. She would have gladly spent more to wash away the rest of the grime if it were possible. Remembering every detail sent goose bumps down her back.

Temple fell out of the crowd and landed with a thud next to her.

"Where have you been?" she asked.

"I stopped to bury our cat . . . the poor little thing deserved it. Can you believe how crowded this place is? When's the President coming out?" He turned around and eyed the man behind him. Someone had elbowed him in the back.

"Any minute now. How do I look?" she asked hopefully. Buttoning her jacket had covered the dirty blouse, but there was no hiding the muddy knees or the dirt ground into her hair. She didn't want the President to think she was a ragamuffin.

"Really awful," he said.

Her heart sank at hearing those words. That was the one thing she both loved and hated about Temple. His honesty. She hated the hurtful things but knew he told the truth—not in a mean sort of way, but in an honest sort of way. She knew if he said a school project was good, it was really good. And she also knew if he said it was bad, it needed more work—maybe a lot more work. That also meant she must have looked really revolting.

The woman standing next to her smiled. She looked like a model from a beauty magazine. Her perfectly drawn eyebrows hovered like two golden arches above her face. Her fashionable red dress stood out in the crowd. But it was the hair that really caught Erin's eyes. It was so stiff that it stayed in place when she moved. When the woman leaned over to pick up her pencil, her hair stayed in a perfect upside-down flip. This had to be an important woman, Erin decided.

"Are you here to see the President?" the woman asked in a pleasant tone.

Erin gulped at the sound of the woman's voice. It was the same voice used by horrible people when they spoke in front of her parents. It was a voice used to fool her parents into thinking the speaker was actually nice. It was the very tone used by the ice cream man. He would yell at the kids, call them snotty-nosed punks, and then pat them sweetly on the head and speak in that tone of voice when a parent appeared. She didn't trust anyone who talked like that. And she certainly didn't trust anyone with stiff hair.

"Why are you here, honey?" the woman asked again. Her red lipstick outlined perfectly straight teeth.

"I'm here to interview the President. I'm running for class president myself, and I wanted to ask him questions about his job."

"Oh, really?" replied the woman with a chuckle. "How sweet. And who is your father, dear?"

Erin didn't know what to say.

"Is he the mayor . . . or maybe a senator? Perhaps he owns a newspaper? Or has your family contributed money to the campaign?" asked the woman politely. Her long, polished fingernails tapped lightly against the portable telephone in her hand.

"No," answered Erin. "My father is an office manager, but my grandfather used to be a termite inspector. And he used to spray the mayor's house."

The woman's eyes narrowed. "Oh . . . well, perhaps you attend the private boarding school in town."

"No, I go to Franklin Elementary. Mrs. Brambles is my teacher."

"Oh, the *public* school," said the woman, slowly dragging out the word "public." The last syllable rolled out like a hiss.

Erin suddenly felt very uncomfortable. The woman's large grin hadn't changed, but her eyes started to scan Erin's jacket. They stopped and studied her tangled hair and then dropped down to her clean-but-scraped-up hands and disgusting knees. The smile never changed, but the tone of her voice became edgy. Erin wasn't sure what to think. This woman wasn't like the ice cream man at all. The ice cream man only smiled when a parent was around, and he didn't care what clothes you wore.

"Are you with a parent, dear?" whispered the woman.

"No, just my best friend, Temple. He's the sixth-grader on the other side of me. He's here to see the President, too. His class isn't doing a project on democracy like mine, though."

"Well, honey, I'm afraid you can't see the President. The President is a very important man—there are a lot of people waiting for him. These are very important people with important needs, something a youngster wouldn't really understand. Any one of these reporters," she said, waving at the people behind them, "would do anything to have a few words with him. And I really do mean anything. I'm afraid you aren't important enough . . . you are just a little girl.

"You see, children don't vote, now do they? That means they can't hurt him. They don't have money . . . except for some measly pocket money . . . and that means they don't contribute to his salary or his campaign. The national polls aren't interested in kids, so he isn't afraid of you. Quite frankly, you don't have any clout. You are simply invisible . . . IN OTHER WORDS MOVE IT SO SOMEBODY IMPORTANT CAN GET IN!"

Erin sprang back in surprise. The woman's bright red smile had disappeared. Her tightly clenched mouth suddenly became pitted in deep grooves. Underneath her crooked lips stood a row of razor-sharp teeth. The stiff strands of perfectly coiffed hair snapped free with a mighty pop. One by one they uncoiled to create a giant, frizzy bird's nest. What was once a pert nose was now stretched into a carrot-shaped point. The woman's pencil-drawn eyebrows had transformed into two woolly caterpillars and hovered in midair. The once-lovely eyes had narrowed into tiny little slits, with flames of red fire licking out around the eyelashes. The pitch-black pupils spit long beams of poisonous venom into the air. Erin shuddered at the hideous form taking shape. Even Charlotte Pillman couldn't match this woman, and Charlotte Pillman was good—really good.

Erin closed her eyes and summoned up her courage. "I believe I'll stay, thank you very much," she replied stubbornly. Presidents do not run, she told herself. Presidents are not afraid of hags with funny eyebrows and venomous eyes.

Thankful for Temple, she locked onto his arm, and holding on with all her might, she faced the woman again. But to her surprise, the face was no longer that of a witch. She glanced down at the woman's high-heeled shoes. They were perfectly polished pumps. Not the black pointed boots with the red and white-striped stockings she had expected. The witch had returned to human form. Turning away from the strange woman again, she snuggled up against her close friend and faced forward.

Suddenly, the crowd started to applaud. A small group of people walked across the stage, waving to the ecstatic crowd. The people roared. The governor, the mayor and the senator stepped off to the side. The manager of the mine joined them. Then the President of the United States, together with his wife, walked forward. The applause grew louder.The President picked up the microphone. "Good morning, ladies and gentle-man. I am very honored to be here this morning in this lovely town, in

this wonderful state. This is truly a town full of warm and gracious people
. . . and I must say, it was a treat to be greeted by one of your children
with the town photographer this morning. It was only fitting to be interviewed by such a charming young man who, himself, is running for president—president of his fifth-grade class."

Erin froze in place. What was the President saying?

The reporters wrote furiously. A mass of cameras scrambled to
take the perfect shot. The crowd "awed" its appreciation. A long
microphone bobbed above Erin's head. An even longer microphone
accidentally hit Temple in the face. He batted it away with a hand.

As soon the President began to speak again, the crowd became
silent. "This young man asked me, how do I take care of all the people—
the rich, the poor, the hard working, the disabled, the discouraged? How
do I judge which problems are most important? How do I deal with
foreign countries? How do I decide which person does the important
jobs? How do I decide when to use U.S. troops? And how do I decide
which ideas should be laws . . . " He stopped and grinned. "As you can
tell folks, this boy can really ask the questions!"

The crowd laughed.

Temple shook his head in disbelief with each new word. A tear
trickled down Erin's cheek as a rush of reporters pushed against her.
The stream of tears turned to wet dots on the front of her jacket. She
couldn't believe her ears. Billy Perez had beaten her again. Billy Perez
had met the President.

It wasn't fair, she sobbed to herself. She would have asked the
same questions if she had been allowed. And she would have asked him
about the economy, something Billy didn't do. They had learned in current
events that a strong economy meant a strong country. And she wanted
to talk about chemicals in the food. But most important, she wanted to
tell him about her idea to organize a school volunteer team for the
community. The children always said they were bored, and the teenagers
were always hanging around the mall with nothing to do. Erin couldn't
understand why. Who had time to be bored when there were so many
things to do?

Their school desperately needed painting. A white sale would raise the money for the paint, and there were always parents willing to help. There were other projects, too, like replacing trees that had been cut down with new saplings . . . and the senior citizens needed help with their yards . . . and the shelters needed clothes to be collected . . . and the soup kitchens needed people to cook and serve . . . and there were gardens to plant and needy children to teach. There was trash to be picked up and playgrounds to design. Erin continued to sob quietly. Her heart was bursting with things to say.

The President was quiet as he viewed the crowd. "I must say, ladies and gentleman, I am very impressed with the quality of citizenship being taught here today. When I was young, I was only concerned with Sarah Seymour's pigtails. I had not yet grasped the true nature of life. Keep an eye on this boy, Billy Perez. This boy is special. He's a natural-born leader, and I expect him to take on an important role someday . . . "

Erin raised her hand and waved. It was the only chance she had of meeting the President. If only he saw her, if only he knew she was Billy's opponent, he would talk to her! He had to understand she too had questions, she too had ideas . . . she too wanted to be president. She had to get his attention!

She jumped, stretching higher and higher. Temple lifted her high in the air, like a cheerleader. She reached high above the crowd, high above the microphones, high above the cameras. She reached to the sky and waved with every once of her energy.

Finally she was certain the President saw her. She was certain he had turned his head to talk to her. She was certain he . . . but her thoughts were cut short. An advancing crowd knocked Temple off his feet, and she fell to the ground. The crowd continued to push forward with a powerful thrust. Temple disappeared, leaving her helpless among the feet. She struggled to get up, only to be kicked, poked and gouged. A finger caught her eye just as she started to stand. A camera flattened her nose, her face was mashed against someone's back, and a purse rammed into her side. She tucked her head down and shoved with all her might. She was trapped inside a stormy sea of determined people.

THIRTEEN

THE NEW POSTER

Mrs. Brambles called the class to attention. She held the weekly newspaper in her hands. "**Local Boy Charms President of the United States**" it proclaimed across the top in bold letters. Underneath appeared a photograph of Billy Perez shaking hands with the President of the United States. Part of Billy's face had been chopped off to make room for a full frontal view of the President, his presidential grin filling most of the page, but even in the tiny corner where Billy's face was barely visible, Erin could see the pride in his eyes.

Mrs. Brambles read the newspaper article out loud. Erin clicked her Coca-Cola pen and started writing, knowing that the teacher wouldn't mind, as long as she listened and didn't distract the others. After all, Erin had been at the rally, so the story would not benefit her as it would the rest of the class—and she had something very important to do.

She tore out the first piece of notebook paper and wadded it up. Mistakes made in ink were impossible to erase, and it was important for this letter to be perfect. Her correspondence had to be the work of a class leader, and that meant proper paragraphs, correct spelling and her very best cursive. Straightening herself up, she began again.

"Are there any questions for Billy?" asked Mrs. Brambles at the end of the article.

"Were you nervous?" asked Tom in the second row.

Delighted to be of service, Billy scrambled to the front of the classroom. He recited every detail of the rally, totally forgetting to mention that Erin had been there, too. As an actor, Billy was the best. He walked back and forth demonstrating every point. His voice changed with each new person in the story. The President's voice was a low baritone and the mayor's a high tenor. He reminded everyone that he had written each and every question. Then he answered every one of those questions in the President's royal baritone voice. He repeated that part again, just in case someone wasn't listening.

Erin scoffed. Billy Perez was shameless.

She finished the letter, signed her name at the bottom and added the words "Presidential Candidate" underneath. Satisfied that it was the best it could be, she slipped it between two books inside her backpack. The books would protect it from being mutilated, and Grandfather would make sure the postman took it to the post office.

The desk next to her had been calm lately. Charlotte hadn't been kicking her chair or knocking her pencils to the floor. She hadn't tossed Erin's coat around or tried tripping her when she passed. It was unusual, the way Charlotte sat silently in her seat, minding her own business. Erin noticed the same dirty spots on the same clothes day after day. And the matted and stringy hair didn't look like it had been washed in weeks. To make matters worse, Charlotte had been coming in late every morning.

Erin wanted to help if she could, but didn't know what to do. Everything she said and did was upsetting to Charlotte. Charlotte's homework was never done, and she snapped at anyone who noticed. The homework chart was filled with circles next to her name. Her head was down on the desk a good portion of the day, and she cried easily. That just wasn't like Charlotte. Even though Charlotte was a class bully and a terrible neighbor, she had always tried hard in school. She had memorized the American Constitution before anyone else, had picked out the hardest books on the reading list and had always made one hundred percent on her spelling tests. But these days, Charlotte just stared straight ahead.

"Charlotte, want to do the math challenge together?" whispered Erin. She loved the math challenge and couldn't wait for it to be passed out each week. Mrs. Brambles had just given it to Billy to hand out.

Charlotte turned and stared. "You think I want *your* help, Miss Goody Two Shoes? I don't need anybody's help, especially not yours."

The laser beams started attacking. Erin sank down in her chair as the beams grew hotter and hotter, trying to fry her alive. Charlotte growled under her breath. Oily hair hung in front of her sad, angry eyes. Her lips turned up in a snarl.

Erin held her shoulders back and sat up. "I am not a Goody Two

Shoes. Temple says I talk too much and I'm silly. And my grandfather says I can be tenacious. Mrs. Brambles says I don't pay enough attention to my science lessons, and right now Billy Perez is beating me in the race for president."

Charlotte cocked her head to one side and turned away in disgust.

Erin sank down in her seat again and murmured to herself. Charlotte Pillman really hated her, whether she did anything or not. It didn't take much. All she had to do was exist. Just sitting quietly at her desk was enough to get her in trouble. What madness had driven her to speak to Charlotte in the first place? Why couldn't she have just enjoyed the peace and quiet?

"Class," began the teacher, "now that we've finished with current events, I would like to show you the new poster Erin brought in. This one will be replacing her old one. Erin, please stand and tell the class about the new poster."

Erin gulped. Mrs. Brambles had never mentioned she would be giving a speech. She was unprepared! She had only meant to replace the old poster on the wall. Her heart started to pound. The class stared at her, and she could feel her cheeks growing red. The boy with the red hair in the second row opened a notebook and took out a pen. He was the class reporter and would repeat what she said in the school newspaper. Charlotte Pillman drilled her with a second set of laser beams. The boys surrounding Billy doubled over with laughter. Mrs. Brambles smiled, waiting for Erin to stand, while the noise grew louder in the back row. Mrs. Brambles cleared her throat as a warning. Billy folded his arms and leaned back, and the boys stopped giggling.

Erin moved to the front of the room and smiled before holding up the new poster. The new one was made on a fresh piece of white poster board and decorated with black permanent marker. She had spent hours perfecting this one, even setting it out all night to dry. Then she had begged Grandpa to drive her to school, so the corners wouldn't bend in her backpack. That was a mistake she didn't want to happen again. Her father didn't own a printing shop like her opponent, but that didn't matter now because this poster was the real thing. It was exactly what her campaign needed.

Erin Olson wants to be your Class President
She not only cares, but listens
Listens to the voice of All the people

"Tell us why you wanted to change your poster, dear," asked Mrs. Brambles with a twinkle.

"Well," she replied slowly, "I went to the campaign rally this weekend to interview the President, just like Billy, except, I didn't have a newspaper photographer with me. My grandfather had given me a press pass—that is a badge that lets you stand with the reporters. I waited for a chance to interview the President too. I had a whole list of questions I wanted to ask him, but I was told he would never talk to me."

She placed the poster against the blackboard so all the children could see it.

"I don't think the President knew I was there," she said after turning back toward the class. "There were hundreds of reporters with cameras. One man said I wasn't important enough because I didn't vote . . . and because my family wasn't rich . . . "

Mrs. Brambles interrupted. "Who told you these things? Someone said you weren't important enough to talk to the President? Were these the President's people?"

Mrs. Brambles hushed the class. Erin drew in a breath, not knowing what to say. The teacher was angry, and Mrs. Brambles had never been angry with Erin before. She had said something terribly wrong to make Mrs. Brambles so upset—only she didn't know what it was.

Choosing her words more carefully, Erin answered, "There was a woman with stiff hair and a man with a red tie in the press section. They acted nice but told me I was a child and that only rich and important people were allowed to talk with the President . . . or maybe you could see him if you were with a newspaper or a television station because the

President really loved having his picture taken. Billy took a photographer with him, and he was allowed to talk to the President."

Mrs. Brambles acted more disturbed than before. Erin didn't know whether to quit or not. Maybe she thought Erin was making up excuses for not getting an interview with the President. That was why Erin mentioned Billy bringing a photographer. Grandfather said bringing a photographer had guaranteed Billy an interview. If she had known that, she would have brought a photographer too.

"I am not pleased at the way you have been treated. This is disgraceful and I am going to write a letter to the Editor voicing my absolute displeasure. You have every right to be present at that rally and to ask the President anything you like. Now, you go ahead dear and tell us why you changed your poster." Mrs. Brambles strained to speak in a gentle voice.

Erin breathed a sigh of relief. Mrs. Brambles wasn't angry with her after all. Charlotte scribbled on her desk, waiting. The boys in the back row were still. Billy stared at her with intense eyes. The class was quiet. She had everyone's undivided attention. Any worry she had felt soon disappeared. Things had gotten easier once she started.

"I changed my poster because I know I can only be a good class president because I am part of the class. When you are part of a class, you see and feel everything (she was tempted to say that's how she knows Billy is a big sneak but didn't think it wise to say so) . . . and because I know what the problems are, I can help fix them. Good leaders look for solutions, and if one solution doesn't work, then they try another one. You keep working on it until you find something that does work. And my grandfather says it's the caring that really counts in life . . . if you really care for people, that means you also listen to them. I would listen to everyone, no matter who they are."

Glancing down at Charlotte Pillman, Erin thought how she would even listen to her. She continued with a new sense of pride. "Good leaders love the people they hope to lead, like a family."

Mrs. Brambles beamed. The class applauded and Billy held his thumb up in approval. Then he jumped to his feet and shouted, "Well done!" His applause rose above the noise.

Surprised at the response, Erin sat down with a smile. A jovial Mrs. Brambles bounced to the front of the room and pinned up the new poster. Billy continued to cheer and even Charlotte managed a tiny smile. The redhead in the second row winked at her as he wrote the newspaper piece. Feeling electrified, she took out her math homework and turned to the page on fractions. For the first time in the campaign she had said something right.

FOURTEEN

THE COPY CAT

The porch swing glided back and forth as Erin leaned lazily against the wooden slats. The bright autumn leaves tumbled across the yard in puffs of swishing air. Teddy lay across her lap, purring loudly as she stroked his back. His purrs grew more content when she scratched beneath his chin. Teddy was the perfect companion: happy, affectionate and full of attention. But best of all, he was a good listener. Every time she talked, his ears stood straight up. Today she told him all about the cemetery, the Chinese boxes, the mine and the locket. And she told him about Billy Perez—especially about Billy Perez.

It was odd how she remembered things when telling her stories out loud. In the mine, she hadn't remembered that the locket wasn't in her jewelry box, but stored under her bed inside a flat storage box. But as she told Teddy about it, she remembered she had hidden it from her curious cousin, Nicole, the jewelry hound. That meant Billy had not only broken into her bedroom, but snooped through her personal things too. And that was really dirty politics. As soon as she could prove it, she was going to complain to the teacher.

But she didn't understand how he had gotten into her room in the first place. The oak tree was too far from the window ledge, and she had tried jumping to the closest branch just last week. She had chickened out at the last minute after looking down. It was a long, long drop to the bottom, and only Spiderman would have been able to shinny up the side of her house. But she knew Billy was a daredevil and wouldn't put it past him. As her grandfather would say, "Where there's a will, there's a way."

Teddy opened his golden eyes and meowed softly.

Temple strolled up the front sidewalk and took a seat next to her. "I just left Billy Perez at school. The *Sun Chronicle* was interviewing him, and a photographer was waiting to take his picture. He was standing beside his poster. What happened in class today?"

Erin wasn't happy to hear that Billy was being interviewed by the district newspaper. That put him in the paper twice, and she hadn't even been in once. Then she recalled the day silently to herself: the campaign had gone well . . . the students had loved her ideas . . . Mrs. Brambles had been pleased with her new and improved poster . . . she had broken her own record walking home . . . and she had taken out the neighbor's trash. Of course Edna had tried to pay her, but Erin had refused. Yes, she thought, it had been a good day and there wasn't anything to worry about.

"Well," she began, "Mrs. Brambles asked me to tell the class about my new poster . . . that was after Billy told everyone about talking to the President. He made it sound like he and the President were best friends. So, when it was my turn, I told the class if I were president I would listen to everyone, because that is how a leader understands what the people need. That is how a president shows he or she cares."

Temple stared uneasily at the toes of his shoes. "Those were the exact words Billy used when talking to the reporter. He said a good president really listens to the people. He said listening is part of caring and caring is what a president is all about. He finished by saying, 'Good leaders love the people like a family.'"

Erin's hand hovered over Teddy's back. "What!"

Her friend looked terribly depressed at what he was going to say next. "And Billy gave the reporters a new slogan. 'Billy Perez, The Presidential Candidate Who Cares, Who Listens, Then Acts for the Good of all the People.'"

"Really cares, really listens!" protested Erin in a loud voice. Teddy sprang into the air and disappeared. "That was the summary of my entire talk today! Billy Perez copied everything I said. Argghh!"

"Yep, he sounds like he copies to me," her friend said sympathetically. "And you know what the real problem is? No one will remember you said it first."

Teddy's head reappeared at the side of the house.

Jumping to her feet, Erin stomped across the porch in a fury. "After I finished talking to the class, Billy announced in a big, grand voice,

'Well done'. I knew he wasn't to be trusted—I knew it was some sort of trick. He took exactly what I said and used it for himself. He cheated again, Temple. He's a copy cat."

Temple looked as miserable as Erin. "I know . . . but that happens in real campaigns too. I've seen it happen. One person comes up with a great idea, and the next thing you know, the other candidates are using it for themselves. My father says the people don't care who came up with it first."

Erin was really furious now. Billy had taken everything she had said and had taken the credit for himself. He had stolen her golden moment in the sun. He had stomped on her victory. He had pulled another scam out of his book of dirty tricks. Just thinking about it made her blood boil.

"Oh and Rin . . . I saw Bernard following you down the hall today. The weasel had stolen your old poster from the trash can. Did you know he watches your every move? I wouldn't trust him if I were you," teased her friend. "He *luuves* you."

She stared straight ahead. Temple tried to get her attention by passing a hand across her face but she didn't flinch. He tried nudging her side, but she didn't move.

"Come on, cheer up, Rinny; it isn't that bad . . . you still have time to turn things around. This campaign has become exciting. Sure, Billy has good ideas, but so do you. Don't give up—he'll win for sure if you do."

Her eyes narrowed but she didn't move.

Temple gave her a big squeeze. "All the kids are talking about the campaign. That's what you want. It isn't every day the President comes to town and talks to one of the fifth-grade students. I'm sure sorry it wasn't you . . . but the newspaper is giving interviews and taking pictures. This class assignment has turned into the real thing, a real campaign. Everyone is watching and waiting . . . and that's good."

Teddy crept onto the porch and rubbed against Erin's legs. She looked down. Maybe Temple was right, she thought. The campaign wasn't over. The students already knew what kind of people both she and Billy were. The problem was that Billy was cleverer than she realized. She returned to her seat.

The swing made a soft creaking sound as it rocked. A small pocket of leaves spun around in a whirlwind. Teddy jumped up on her lap again as large drops of rain began to fall. Gathering clouds started to rumble above. They sat there quietly as the rain fell.

"Do you still want to go to the Haggerty house tonight?" asked Temple. "It looks like it's going to pour."

"Yes; we need to get to the bottom of these clues. It is more important than ever to catch Billy now," she answered. "I don't care if we have to swim there."

FIFTEEN

RUMORS

Erin waited on the porch for Temple to return with his rain gear. She pulled on her boots and buttoned up her raincoat. The sky had darkened as the dense clouds covered the sun. Enormous sheets of rain fell across the ground. Rain splattered across the wooden floorboards and gathered into little pools of water. Her skin tingled with the dampness. She loved the smell of water in the air.

Temple kicked through the puddles gathering on the sidewalk and walked up the steps. "You sure about us going to the Haggerty Mansion? You know what they say about that place . . . that's its haunted. And I have a new one for you . . . the barber says you can hear moans coming from the stone tower during a full moon. Seems Miss Haggerty was engaged once but something happened, and they say instead of marrying him, she chained him to the walls. It's supposed to be his ghost crying out in the night."

Lightening streaked against the sky.

Temple laughed. "And . . . my uncle thinks Miss Haggerty is related to Bluebeard the Pirate. Rumors say he buried his treasure under the cellar and filled the pit with the bones of fortune hunters."

"Grandfather says those are just rumors," Erin said. "Do you believe them?"

"Yea, sort of." Temple smirked. "I mean something must have happened for people to start talking. What about you?"

"You're probably right." She buttoned the top of her raincoat. The wind was twisting her hair into knots as she tried to push it inside her hat.

A car riding parallel to the sidewalk, stopped in front of them. A hand pushed a plastic-covered newspaper out the window. Umbrellas open, Erin and Temple jumped down the steps. The man handed the bundle to Erin. "Oy, you going out in weather like this Miss?"

"We've got business with Miss Haggerty," Erin said from underneath the rim of her umbrella.

"The Haggerty Mansion! Crikey! I wouldn't go there miss. The old lady's crackers you know. Why just a fortnight ago someone went missing . . . poor bloke was delivering an odd parcel of herbs and spices . . . you know the sort you hear about in potions and spells. The old crone wanted some eye of newt! Can you imagine? Poor little newts having their eyes pried out for the likes of her. The poor bloke wouldn't of gone, knowing the kind of person she was, but he was desperate—why with his mum needing medicine and all . . ."

The man spoke through a partially opened window as the rain poured in through the crack.

"It was a night same as this but worse . . . the likes you've never seen . . . the thunders a cracking and the rain cutting the skin like razors . . . but he goes out anyway. He should have minded the first omen. Borrows a car he does, and the bloody thing won't start . . . never done that before, mind you. Well, with a little know-how he gets the thing a going, but he's sopping wet by this time. When you're working under the bonnet, you're not worried about getting wet, and his mum needed the medicine and all. Then he gets a flat—and the car with new tires! He should have turned around right there and then . . . but no, his mum needs her medicine, and he's a good lad, so he changes the tire and heads off." The man shuddered.

The storm raged. A solid wall of rain erupted, wildly pounding against the ground. Water-drenched mounds of leaves became matted and lifeless. A river of water formed along the sidewalk. Lightening crackled against a purple—almost black—sky. Erin began to shiver. Temple prodded her in the side. "Still want to go?"

She nodded yes miserably.

"Wait!" said the man, his face twisted in agony. "I ain't, finished yet . . . that's only the leading-up line. You ain't heard the best part. The bloke, now sopping wet and shivering to beat the band, arrives at the mansion . . . the lights is off and the driveway pitch black. It's a good thing me headlights is workin', the bloke thinks to himself, or I'd be blinder than a headless horseman. No sooner do the words pass his lips, than a crack of lightening rips across the sky and sends the ground rocking. And what do you think happens next? Hiz headlights pop, and quits altogether. It's suddenly pitch black and the bloke can't see!"

Temple tried to muffle the concern in his voice. "Is this really true, Mr. Doyle?"

"I swear on my dead brother's grave, I do. It was told to me by the sister of the butcher . . . and she said, he said, a customer told him . . . who heard it from his misses (a woman of great character) that it's all in black and white down at the police station where she cleans at nights."

Erin and Temple both said, "Oohh . . . ." at the same time.

Another crack of lightening streaked in the background.

"So like I was saying . . . Here's this bloke standing in the dark. He's got eye of newt in the car—the stuff is finicky and can't be out of the icebox for long . . . He can't go back 'cause he can't drive the car with no headlights, so he has to go forward. It's off to the mansion, he goes, whether he likes it or not. Well, the lightening is flashing across the sky, and it helps him see the mansion . . . so he starts heading for the outline. He can't see the ground and there's some awful bad ruts down there. He's tripping and cursing and wishing he could just close his eyes and the whole thing would go away . . . but he can't because he's really doing it—it ain't no dream he can wake up from . . .

"He steps on something that feels like a dead body but he can't see, and he doesn't want to be sticking hiz hands down there to find out. It's bad enough being drenched to the bone; he doesn't really want to know if there's a body there . . . 'cause that would change things for the worse, and he's already feeling things are bad enough . . . so he keeps on going. The lightening is hissing and snapping and showing him the way to the front door."

He stopped and stared at them, waiting.

"Well?" Erin asked anxiously. "What happened?"

The man chuckled. "I was just waiting to see if you was interested . . . I guess you are. So, anyway, he stumbles up to the door and knocks . . . mind you, this is a heavy door and he's pounding as hard as a man can. No one answers! Not wanting to leave, he opens the door. There's candles everywhere, and he calls out hoping someone would come . . . No one comes. Well, he doesn't know what to do—should he go in or leave. He's thinking hard, and then remembers his poor old mum waiting at home for her medicine . . . So he calls out again, and still no one answers. He makes his way to the kitchen, and that's where he saw it . . . made his bones shiver it did. He's just standing there goggling at the thing when it turns and grins at him, it does. Stretches its swollen lips across a mouth full of rotten teeth . . . "

"What does?" whispers Erin.

"Why the disembodied head! Sitting there in a glass jar is the head of a man, and the man's smiling with a big toothy grin! Hiz face is all splotchy and swollen, and one eye is almost shut, but the man could still smile . . . gives me the creeps that does."

Erin and Temple stared at each other in horror.

"Well, the bloke drops hiz package and runs like the dickens . . . he makes hiz way back to the car, and suddenly everything is working. The headlights come on, the engine is purring like a cat, and nothing is stopping him from driving to freedom. He goes straight to the coppers and tells them what he saw . . . and you know the worst of it? His poor mum gets her medicine but he's disappeared since. Not a trace of him can be found."

"Whoa!" Temple and Erin replied in unison.

"You two sure you want to be visiting Miss Haggerty? Like I said, I swear the story is true on my dead brother's grave. Oh, and by the way . . . give your grandfather me gratitude. Lovely batch of chocolate chips . . . me misses ate every one of them."

Mr. Doyle drove on down the street, tossing bundles out into yards.

"Do you think he really has a dead brother?" Temple asked.

Erin shrugged her shoulders as they pointed their umbrellas into the wind and started slowly toward the mansion.

SIXTEEN

MiSS HaggERTY

It was a long, dark driveway. The old mansion, built like a castle, sat deep inside the property. A bell tower stood in the east wing. The tower's large bells had been silenced over a hundred years ago, upon the arrival of the Haggerty family. Long, chiseled gargoyles hung from the eaves above. Gushing waters from the storm tumbled from their opened mouths like waterfalls. A thick row of dark thunderclouds crackled across the horizon.

Temple and Erin stopped to look at the spectacle before them. Erin tilted forward and peered out from under the rim of her rain-washed umbrella. Large streams of water fell from the edge and splattered across her boots. She felt inside her pocket. The locket and the secret weapon were tucked safely away. She didn't know why she had bothered to bring the secret weapon. It had been of no use in the cemetery, but knowing it was close made her feel safer, anyway.

Large gullies of water covered the path. A faint glow from the windows shined against the dark background. They made their way up to the ivy-covered entrance.

Temple rang the doorbell. "Ow!" he screeched, tipping back awkwardly in his boots. "That doorbell shocked me! It burns!"

He held his index finger up in the air. Erin examined the injured tip and then checked the door. The bell looked like an ordinary doorbell. There were no exposed wires or loose-fitting parts. As a matter of fact, it looked brand new.

A clanking noise came from the other side of the door. It opened. Against a flickering, weak light stood a hunched figure; bent at the shoulders. A long, thin arm gripped a parrot's head on top of a twisted cane. The parrot's red eyes sparkled in the light. A limp black dress hung above the woman's pointed shoes. A tightened belt revealed the thin waist of a frail woman.

Gray hair, pulled loosely to the top of her head, coiled around like a serpent. The large, hooked nose resembled a parrot's beak, and below the silvery eyebrows were coal-black eyes, shimmering against a chalky white face. When the long, slender face smiled, the hollowed cheeks sunk below the bone.

Erin gulped.

"What do you ninnies want?" hissed the old woman.

Feeling for Temple's hand, Erin whispered, "Ninny?" in her lowest possible tone.

"A fool, a simpleton," he whispered back.

"Madam Haggerty," interjected a deep, booming voice from behind the door. "Perhaps I can help with the guests."

"Go away, Winston," barked the woman, shooing away an invisible person. "I can handle these little brats—got them with my electric doorbell already. This ugly boy just got a good bolt of juice. Did that shock feel good, my little urchin?" She leaned forward and stared directly into Temple's eyes.

Temple's head moved up and down slowly, as if in a trance.

"That'll teach you to pester me," she snapped with a chuckle.

Breaking free from the trance, Temple pushed Erin's hand away and stepped forward. "That doorbell is electrified . . . and you shocked me on purpose? I could have been electrocuted!"

"Oh, stop whimpering, you little toad," scolded the woman. "It is so unbecoming to complain. The current cuts off after half a second." Raising the cane high above her head, she brought it down with a whack across his legs.

"Ow!" shrieked Temple, grabbing his ankle with his injured hand. His body teetered back and forth as he tried to catch his balance.

The old woman lifted her cane and placed the tip against his shoulder. With a sharp hiss, she pushed forward with a mighty lunge. Temple fell over backwards, landing like a turtle on his back. The woman cackled out loud.

Erin couldn't believe what she had just seen. Throwing herself between the old woman and her friend, she screamed, "Miss Haggerty, please!"

The cane came down again, pounding the toe area of Erin's boot. "Ouch!" she cried.

A voice from behind the door, interrupted. "Really, madam, do you think it wise to antagonize our guests like this? These are children . . . and they don't appear to be up to any mischief. If you would kindly let me talk to these youngsters, perhaps we could handle this matter in a more amiable fashion."

Erin backed away from the entrance. "Miss Haggerty, my name is Erin Olson and I'm here to ask a question. We don't want to annoy you. Please, we need only a moment."

"Hogwash and rubbish," muttered the woman. "All children are demons . . . little worms digging through the ground. They pick your flowers and torture the cat . . . they put nasty notes on the door and throw eggs at your windows. They dump garbage on the sidewalk and call you indecent names. I hate little children . . . little children just like you." Then she hissed and limped away.

Erin stared in disbelief at the empty doorway. Temple hobbled forward, trying to see inside the shadowy hallway. A tall, elderly man stepped out from the shadows and blocked the view.

"Winston is my name. I am madam's butler. Miss Haggerty is feeling a little feisty today, and I must apologize. Please, do come in out of this nasty bit of weather, and tell me how I can help."

Stepping aside, he motioned for them to enter.

iNSiDE THE HaUNTED MaNSiON

Lightning streaked across the sky. The bright light flashed against the stained glass windows, and the thunder crashed seconds later. Erin removed her wet raincoat and placed it on the antique hall tree. A large puddle grew around the folded umbrellas propped against the wall. The muddy boots stood alongside the wall. Temple struggled to pull off his wet parka. Winston waited with chin forward and fingertips tucked neatly inside his vest pockets.

The foyer glimmered from the flickering lights of the oil lanterns. A row of dimly lit portraits hung throughout the long and narrow hallway. Erin glanced from portrait to portrait. The family resemblance was strong. Each portrayed coal-black eyes, a pale complexion and a hooked nose pointing up with an air of superiority.

"Madam is waiting in the drawing room. Please follow me," announced the butler.

Erin turned nervously toward her friend, noticing his wide eyes and curious expression. Temple had always wanted to explore the Haggerty mansion just like all the children in town. He knew every story relating to the house. Up until this evening she hadn't really cared, but now things had changed. She reached for his hand and led him forward.

The house was old and dark. Blood-red walls stretched into endless hallways. Stamped copper panels hung from the ceiling above. The eyes of the portraits moved as the threesome passed through the hallway. Tall, thin flames danced inside the mounted lanterns, casting shadows against the twelve-foot walls. With every turn, they were greeted by strange and ghostly shapes.

Winston walked cautiously down the corridor, his long, slender legs moving purposefully, as if never in a hurry. He turned and motioned straight ahead. The lantern at his side swung back and forth, its flickering light dancing along the walls. The thunder cracked violently above. Erin squeezed Temple's hand. His wide-open eyes continued to comb the passageway. The butler stopped at a large arched doorway and motioned for them to enter.

The roaring fire glowed, its warmth drying the chilly air. Temple stepped into the open chamber, but Erin paused. Next to the fireplace, perched like a buzzard, sat old lady Haggerty. The knotted cane was only inches from her hands. The parrot's red eyes appeared to swirl like two pools of molten lava in the flickering light. Temple tried to pull Erin forward, but she wouldn't move. There was something peculiar about the old woman's eyes. Foul, red rims outlined the coal-black centers. The glint of evil sparkled in the firelight.

"Sit down," cackled the old woman. Her long, bony fingers pointed at a nearby cushion.

Temple gave Erin another tug, moving her reluctantly toward the sofa. She hovered nervously above the cushion. Her eyes searched the doorway and the walls first. The room had two doors to adjoining rooms entering at different points. If anything happened, she knew there was more than one way out. She sat down with great apprehension.

But then she suddenly sprang to her feet. Temple rocked forward when her weight bounced off the cushions. "Huhh . . . " she groaned. Her eyes filled with tears. Gingerly reaching behind her, she found it. A round silver object was sticking out of the seat of her pants. "Look at this gi . . . gigantic thumbtack!" she squealed. The large thumbtack flashed in the firelight as she showed it to Temple.

The old woman strummed her fingers together in delight—her twinkling black eyes fluttering with excitement. Her thin, weathered lips curled up, and her eyebrows twitched when she cackled silently to herself. "Something wrong, my dear?" she mused.

Erin blinked back her tears, even though she wanted to cry. Presidents don't cry, she told herself, even over a gigantic thumbtack planted on the seat cushion by a retched old woman. Holding her head high, she managed to smile politely. She felt every inch of the cushion before sitting down again like a perfect lady.

Miss Haggerty snorted.

Erin folded her hands delicately across her lap, and pretended nothing had happened. She didn't want to give Miss Haggerty the satisfaction.

The room was warm and cozy. Antiques lined the walls. A lion's head hung on one wall, a trophy from a distant safari. In front of the fireplace lay a tiger-skin rug. Rows of books sat upon the shelves. The window's long, flowing drapes lay in folds against the floor.

The old woman smiled. "Well, my dears, it is so nice to have visitors. We at the *haunted mansion* rarely have visitors. At least live ones," she sniggered.

Erin drew in a breath, trying hard to look unconcerned.

"You see we do like company, especially young tender children— the ones without their mamas and daddies around. Why, just the other day, Winston and I had a young boy for lunch," she said softly. A smirk crept across her face. "He was quite delicious, if you understand my meaning."

The old woman cackled, her hands bouncing up and down on her lap with glee. The fire grew instantly bigger, as if fed by a magic puff of wind. But, apparently the effort had been too much. She sat back against the couch and stared straight ahead, her face now expressionless. Winston looked down at his mistress.

Erin's eyes pleaded with her friend. Temple's expression was clear. "Give the sign and we're out of here!" She really didn't know what to do. It was obvious Temple was in agreement. This was not the place to be. In her mind, she retraced their steps back to the front door. It was past the gallery of creepy portraits and what must have been a dungeon entrance. At the very far end of the hallway, stood the heavy door bearing two-inch spikes and iron brackets.

Erin's concentration was broken when the old woman began to stir. Sparks escaped from the fireplace, as it grew hotter and hotter. Miss Haggerty leaned over and picked up a tray from the table next to her. "Ladyfinger, my dear?"

The plates and teacups rattled against the silver tray as the old woman struggled to keep it steady. Erin hesitated. Winston lifted the silver dome covering.

"Go ahead, child, eat your ladyfingers," snapped the woman

anxiously. "You don't want to disappoint an old woman do you?"

The contents looked very strange. These weren't the spongy, cake-like cookies, Erin had expected. They were long sticks of white chocolate—shriveled up, *stale* sticks of white chocolate. These were sticks that couldn't really be called white anymore. They were shriveled up sticks of *dirty* white chocolate with moldy spots. The surface was no longer creamy and yummy-looking, but withered, with cracks running along the surface.

In fact, the four funny-looking sticks of white chocolate didn't look like anything Erin wanted to eat. She scrunched up her nose just *thinking* of placing one in her mouth.

"What's the matter dear…don't care for *lady* fingers?" asked the old woman in a deep, throaty rumble.

Erin stared at the plate, and then at Miss Haggerty.

"Come on, dear, have a tasty bone," said the old woman.

"Do you mean these are *real* fingers?" asked Erin in horror.

"Of course," snapped the old woman. "These are the fingers of Lady Margaret Hargrave. That is the proximal phalanx, that's the middle phalanx and that's the distal phalanx. Strung together, they make up the bones of the finger. The distal phalanx is my personal favorite. It has a crunchy taste all its own. It is better known as the fingertip." She smiled and smacked her lips together after cleaning a tooth with her long fingernail.

Erin looked up in alarm. The plate dropped to the floor. The cylinder-shaped bones bounced across the tiger-skin rug.

"Really, Madam," reminded the butler. "You promised the doctor you wouldn't play with the bones anymore. He is still quite annoyed with you for putting Lady Hargrave's eye in his tea the other day—says it ruined his appetite for a week. Perhaps we should see what the children want." Winston placed the bones back on the silver tray and set the plate off to the side.

Erin slid closer to her trusted friend and wrapped an arm around his.

"Hurry up, Rin, and ask her," whispered Temple. "Let's get out of here."

The old woman snickered. The flames of fire licked against the cold draft from the chimney. The warm glow of light bathed the room, giving a false sense of tranquility. The butler stood motionless by the old woman's side. The parrot's head was poised only inches away.

Erin reached into her pocket and slowly removed the locket. Her hand brushed up against the envelope with the secret weapon. This was the first time she had been tempted to take it out of hiding. But, not wanting to blow their chances of having a few questions answered, she nudged it back down.

Winston urged her to begin.

"Miss Haggerty," she said as politely as she could, "Temple and I found this locket inside the old mine. It was pushed into a hole, down at the bottom of the large shaft. Have you seen this locket before?"

Winston's gloved hand picked up the locket and placed it on the old woman's outstretched palm. Miss Haggerty snapped the case open like an expert. She studied the picture for a long time. "What was your business in the mine?" asked the old woman harshly. "I own the mine and you were trespassing on my property. I should have you little grubs locked up."

"Madam, you sold the mine some years ago," replied the butler. "It is now a living museum, sponsored by the state. Madam was very pleased that the mine was being used for educational purposes."

The old woman motioned for her servant to be quiet.

"Well?" she hissed.

"Searching for a clue," answered Erin, timidly. "I've been receiving mysterious clues that tell me to go to different places. The last clue led us to the mine, and that's where we found this locket . . . only, even though this locket belongs to me, it has your picture in it. Why would your picture be inside my locket, Miss Haggerty?"

"Why should I help you!" snorted the woman, "I'm going to have you arrested for trespassing on mine property! You little heathens have no business there . . . that mine belongs to my family. We took if from the greedy little immigrants years ago. They were peasants who came to this country to get rich . . . they thought they were smart enough to take on the likes of us. But no sirree." Her finger slashed the air several times.

The fire roared in the background, sparks flying high above the flames.

"My family undercut them . . . gave the people cheaper minerals and plenty of 'em, because that's what the people wanted. The mine owners said they couldn't pay their workers and sell the minerals for less, but we sold ours cheaper anyway, even though we lost money. Of course the buyers came to us instead of the mine owners, leaving the mine owners with minerals they couldn't sell and workers they couldn't pay. Hee, hee . . . it took a little while, but we put the mine out of business. Then we bought it for a song. You see, that's how it works, my little imbeciles.

"Money has the power. Don't ever forget that. The person with power can fry you up and eat you for breakfast. Now, who gave you permission to enter my mine?"

Erin searched desperately for an answer.

"Well?" snapped the woman, her fist pounding against the arm of the sofa. Her breaths started coming in short, rapid puffs. The rhythm became more frantic with each passing second.

"Miss Haggerty, please," begged Erin. "We didn't disturb anything in the mine—we left it as we found it. We just need to know if you have ever seen this locket before . . . or the picture. Do you know anything that can help us?"

The old woman stood, raising the cane high above her shoulders. The parrot's head grew larger. The red, glowing eyes began to stir. The yellow pupils grew brighter. Erin reached for Temple's hand. He pushed against the corner of the sofa. The thunder grew to a deafening level outside.

Winston stepped forward from the fireplace and blocked the old woman's path.

"Does Madam require my services?" he asked calmly.

"Winston, step aside immediately," demanded the old woman.

"No, ma'am. I can not," he responded firmly.

The cane came down with a crack on a tall oriental vase. It splintered into tiny shards. "I SAID MOVE ASIDE, WINSTON!"

"No, ma'am. I can not," he repeated softly.

Erin and Temple scrambled to their feet. Miss Haggerty teetered back and forth, waving the cane frantically in the air. Winston stood like a rock as the old woman beat repeatedly against his chest with her free hand. Then she stopped, grunting in despair. The butler pulled his waistcoat into place and patted the old woman gently on the back while whispering softly in her ear. Miss Haggerty lowered the cane. Erin sighed with relief. Temple let out a small whistle. Winston smiled with approval and stepped aside.

Miss Haggerty's head hung as she motioned for them to come closer. Winston waved them forward. The old woman patted Erin affectionately on the arm and placed the locket back in her hand.

Then, with a jerk of her head, she stepped back and motioned with the cane. "Escort these horrid creatures to the dungeon, Winston! Chain them; don't let them go!" roared the tiny woman. Her hand tightened around the parrot's head, and with the speed of lightning, brought the cane down across their legs. "To the dungeon with these little maggots, before they get away."

EIGHTEEN

WINSTON

Grabbing them both by the collar, Winston dragged Erin and Temple, kicking and fighting, past the old woman. Choking under the butler's strong grip, their muffled cries filled the room. Once outside the door, Winston released the squirming guests, letting them flop to the floor from the struggle.

He helped them to their feet and motioned for them to be silent by placing a finger across his lips. Temple angrily pulled his clothes into place. Erin rubbed her injured shins.

The butler led them wordlessly down a long corridor, past a large library and a hallway with an early American grandfather clock. They moved silently, placing one foot ahead of the other on the wooden floorboards. Temple stepped on a loose board. The harsh creaking noise rang through the hall. The three of them became instantly still.

The clock's long hand moved over the Roman numeral three. With a sharp tap of its gears, musical chimes started sounding the quarter hour. The sound reverberated against the ancient walls, sending a sweet melody pouring through the rooms. The music stopped, and the mansion was silent once again.

Winston was the first to move. He glanced in both directions before pointing to an enormous kitchen with a cast iron stove. A long country table surrounded by twelve upright chairs stood in the middle of the room.

"Please, have a seat, children," said the butler, directing them to the chairs furthest from the door. "It is safe in the kitchen. Madam rarely comes here. Of course if Spike, is hungry, she'll occasionally stop by to get him a snack. You've had a most dreadful experience. I'll make some fresh cocoa, and we can chat."

Feeling uneasy, Erin studied the butler's face. He was an elderly gentleman, much younger than his mistress, with thick white hair and a smooth, rosy complexion. His head turned slightly when he talked. His eyes were kind, unlike his mistress'. He didn't seem to be the type to get upset easily. Winston-the-butler was a good man, she decided at last, like her grandfather; he could be trusted.

The storm continued to beat against the rooftop. Erin huddled next to her friend. She didn't know if she was shivering because of Miss Haggerty or because of the storm. Either way, she was chilled to the bone. Goosebumps rose up on her arms.

"Forgive us for your unfortunate ordeal. Of course I simply couldn't stand by and let two innocent children be thrown into that horrendous dungeon." He placed three napkins on the table. "Miss Haggerty is declining, I'm afraid. I believe she has the same touch of madness that afflicted her great grandfather . . . what a bloody pirate he was. It was his blood money that brought riches to the family. I don't approve of blood money, but it spends the same and the family has done well with it."

"We didn't mean to upset Miss Haggerty," Erin whispered. "We didn't know her family owned the mine. We're very grateful for not being thrown into the dungeon. My grandfather would have been very upset if I had let myself get trapped inside something like that."

Temple leaned forward, his voice barely audible. "You mean there really is a dungeon? I've never seen one before."

"Oh, yes," Winston continued, "and I must add, it's a damp and musty old thing. Madam uses the dungeon to produce wine now. But I'm afraid the dungeon does have a bit of a history. During the 1800s, when slavery was still legal in the South, a special section of the dungeon was used to trap runaway slaves. It was a large, stone-lined pit in the ground. The sides were twenty feet down and greased so the slaves couldn't crawl out. Awful place, really. I've often wondered about the people who've been confined there."

Winston let out a long sigh and removed a pot from the rack. "Thank goodness, that is an era long past now." He reached into the pantry and removed a sack of sugar and a container of Hershey's Cocoa."

Erin rubbed her arms. "I love warm cocoa . . . especially the kind made into a paste and mixed with warm milk. That's the only way my grandfather makes it. He says the instant stuff in the stores has no taste."

Winston smiled. "Really? I believe I would like your grandfather."

Erin looked eagerly at the cocoa and then glanced at Temple. The grouchiness had left his face. He was smiling at the prospect of hot cocoa.

Winston took a bright, red-and-black Mickey Mouse apron from the pantry. The large round ears stretched from shoulder to shoulder. The face covered his entire mid-section, with Mickey's round nose settling in the middle. The nose looked like a giant navel. Erin giggled at the picture before her.

The butler placed a pair of reading glasses across his nose and carefully measured the sugar and cocoa. He spoke in a comforting tone. "That picture inside the locket was taken recently by the newspaper, upon Madam's ninety-ninth birthday. I dare say that photograph was everywhere. Your locket appears to hold one of many newspaper clippings. Is that of some use to you, my dear?" He poured the hot mixture into three tall mugs. "Marshmallows?"

They nodded enthusiastically.

"Yes, that explains where the picture came from. Does Miss Haggerty own a locket like this one?" asked Erin. She sipped the gooey marshmallows slowly from the top. A warm feeling started to radiate from inside.

"Madam does not believe in jewelry. There is a small selection stashed away for special occasions, but no lockets. She believes them to be sentimental, and madam does not like to be sentimental. Ever since her intended was killed in a car accident, she has refused to wear such adornments. Is your cocoa satisfactory?" he asked, one eyebrow arched high above the other.

"Yes, thank you . . . but I don't understand. Why would a picture of Miss Haggerty be in my locket? Do you think she knows something but won't tell us?" she asked. The steam hovering above her cup spiraled into the air and disappeared.

"No, Miss. Madam doesn't go out much and doesn't care for strangers as you can tell. Some people refer to her as a recluse. She accepted the newspaper reporter upon my insistence. You see, some people think she has passed on and inquire about such each time I go into the town center. So, when a reporter called and asked for an interview, I felt Miss Haggerty should respond favorably."

Temple set his cocoa down. "So, you think the picture is from the local newspaper and Miss Haggerty was not involved with the clue in the mine?"

"Yes, Mr. Temple, that is what I believe to be true," stated the butler thoughtfully. "But I am curious, Miss Erin. You never mentioned why you are receiving these so-called clues. I would like to hear more, if I may. I'm afraid Miss Haggerty was being a little naughty and not much help. I attend to most of Madam's business and may be able to spread some light."

Erin had been stirring her cocoa. The steam was almost gone, making it the perfect temperature. She set the spoon off to the side. "I'm running for president of my fifth-grade class, and I have a sneaky opponent named Billy Perez. He's been playing a trick on me. He put a dead rat on my doorstep, made me go to the cemetery where he taped a bag over my face, then gave me a riddle telling me to look for a clue in the mine. I know he wants me to run after these clues instead of concentrating on my campaign—but if I ignore the clues, then I won't be able to catch him . . . and I need to prove it's him. I already made the mistake of accusing him in front of the class. Of course, he said he didn't do it, and now everyone is laughing at me."

"I see," said the butler. "Does your opponent happen to be a young boy about your age—a little shorter, with dark hair?"

"Why yes," exclaimed Erin. "Do you know him?"

She leaned anxiously toward the butler. Temple scooted closer.

"You think he is the one sending you the clues?" asked the butler.

"Yes, I do."

"Tonight, before you arrived at the doorstep, I saw a boy following you in the surveillance cameras. I witnessed you and Mr. Temple approaching the grounds, but there was a third figure darting along the bushes. At first, I thought he was one of the local boys coming to torment Madam, but then I noticed he was following your exact footsteps. I got a glimpse of him when you came to the door. He was standing directly behind the topiary bush . . . about your age . . . with dark hair. Mind you, he was soaking wet. He fled after Mr. Temple stuck his finger in the electrified doorbell. Apparently he wasn't interested in staying around after that."

Erin turned toward Temple and squealed with excitement.

"You're absolutely certain of this?" Temple asked.

"Yes, Mr. Temple. I am an elderly man, but my eyesight is perfect. There was a young boy following you and Miss Erin . . . tonight . . . here at the mansion."

Erin tried to grasp everything that had been said. Had Billy hoped she would enter the haunted mansion and never come out? Like a black hole in space? And why did he follow them to the door, then leave? She had suspected he was following them all along but hadn't dared to say so. Her skin tingled when he was around, like a cat sensing a mouse.

Thunder clashed above. A sharp bolt of lightning crackled outside the kitchen window, illuminating a dark and gloomy sky. A sheet of water washed against the glass pane as a distorted silhouette flashed outside the window.

"Temple! Look!" Erin screamed. "It's Billy!"

The lightning cracked again. But only drops of rain streamed against a bare window. Temple and Winston turned toward the door. The sky continued to snap with large bursts of lights. Winston opened the door. The pelting rain blew across the floor.

"I'm sorry, Miss, but there is no one there," he said sadly, closing the door.

"Rinny, you're seeing things again," warned Temple. "If, and I emphasize the word *if*, if Billy Perez were here earlier, he would be gone by now. Whoever was following us was probably one of the neighborhood boys, curious about why we were headed here. And what you saw outside this window was probably the shadow of that big tree. Look at the size of that trunk and those long, thick branches . . . with the wind bending them back and forth, they could easily be mistaken for a person."

"Perhaps Mr. Temple is right," agreed the butler. "It's not unusual for people to make their way across the mansion's grounds. The old house attracts many unwanted visitors."

Erin finished her cocoa and watched the lightning dancing across the sky. Temple had never dealt with anybody like Billy. He had never been up against somebody so cunning. She could understand him thinking she was wrong, but she knew what she saw. And Temple was probably right, Billy would certainly be gone by now."

"Winston," she said softly, trying to change the subject. "Did Miss Haggerty's family really starve out the mine owners?"

Winston looked down. "Miss Haggerty is from a very wealthy family, and money does have power, Miss Erin, even though you are too young to understand. There are ways of doing business that people never talk about. I'm afraid, Miss Haggerty's family was too powerful for the hard working people of the mine."

She pushed her empty cup away. "That wasn't fair."

"Life isn't fair, Miss Erin," replied the butler. He gathered the empty cups from the table and placed them near the sink. "The sooner one realizes that, the sooner one will be able to deal with life. Now, we must conclude our chat. I'm afraid Madam will be checking the halls with her Doberman shortly. Spike is not a dog I relish confronting on the best of terms."

Winston walked them slowly toward the front door. Erin and Temple struggled to put on their wet coverings. The storm continued to beat with fury. Erin focused on the drawing room door, the last place Miss Haggerty had been seen. Little shadows bouncing off the oil lanterns gave her reason for concern. Each one was shaped like a tiny woman with an enormous cane. The shadows crept across the hall like they were stalking an enemy. Every flicker of light caused her to jerk. She hopped helplessly on one foot, frantically wrestling with her wet boots. Finally, she won the battle and stood fully clothed against the storm.

"Well, children, I hope I have been of some help," said the butler. He opened each umbrella, handing the first one to Erin. "Now, Miss, that does remind me. Yesterday, we received a letter addressed to E. Olson at this address. I found it odd that such a name would be addressed here. I had put it aside for the postman, but a thought suddenly occurs to me. Perhaps this letter was intended for you. It seems E. Olson could possibly be Erin Olson. Have a look, and if the letter does not belong to you, please return it to the proper place."

Pulling a tattered pink envelope from the hall table, Winston placed it in Erin's hand.

NINETEEN

THE MYSTERIOUS LETTER

The thunder had stopped by the time Erin and Temple reached the front door of her house. The drenching rain had slowed to a steady drizzle, creating a thin veil of mist. Teddy waited anxiously by the front door, meowing loudly. Erin removed the shoestring from around her neck, slid the house key into the lock and opened the door. Cold and wet, they went inside and headed for the kitchen, where they peeled off their soaked rainwear.

"Since you insist the pink envelope isn't a birthday card, I want to know what it is. Don't make me beg," Temple said sharply. His wet hair hung in ringlets. The water dripping from the ends collected into small pools on the tabletop. A quick swipe from his elbow wiped the drips away. "You just want to torture me. You could have easily read the letter on the way home from the mansion."

Erin opened the letter, laying it flat in front of her. Temple strained for a glance at the pink message. Small, rectangular letters cut from newspaper clippings were glued into rows. Upside down, the words were unrecognizable.

"No, it would have been ruined by the rain, or the wind might have ripped it from my hands—the same way it blew the hat off your head and sent it sailing over the pond and into the woods before you knew what was happening. And my hair was already blowing into knots, so I had to keep a hand on my hat," she said, purposely blocking the message with her shoulder so he couldn't see.

Each time he attempted to look, she raised her shoulders a little higher. She studied the paper cutouts. Some of the letters had been cut from a magazine. The color was rich and made from thick paper. The other letters had been cut from a newspaper. Their colors were faded and the paper-thin. The letters had been trimmed into cubes without any telling marks. None of the pieces contained a newspaper heading. The person making this message had been very selective. The backside of the paper was completely blank.

"Well?" huffed Temple.

"Someone did a really sloppy job of cutting out the letters. They must have used those little kindergarten scissors that tear the paper apart. And what about the pink paper?" she said thoughtfully. "Do you think the color pink has any significance?"

"Because you like pink?" he said sarcastically. He threw up his arms. "How am I supposed to know? You won't let me see it. Now, give it here."

"Do you know anyone with a fingerprinting kit?" she continued. Her mouth curled up in one corner. His rudeness didn't annoy her a bit. He could wait. "We could dust it for fingerprints and dust each letter and the envelope. Some of the letters are loose . . . we could dust the paper under them."

"What good would that do?" snapped Temple. "You think someone this clever would leave fingerprints? Besides, what would we do with them? You need to have a listing of all the fingerprints in existence so you can match them to a person, and we don't have that. We can't just walk into the police station and ask them to identify our little prints lifted from a letter. What makes you think our mystery person has fingerprints on record anyway? Maybe we do have fingerprints, but we have nothing to compare them with." His nostrils were flaring by this time. "Now, what does it say!"

Erin snatched the letter from the table and backed out of reach, eyeing him mischievously. "It's another clue," she whispered, waving the paper in the air.

"No joke . . . stop teasing, and tell me what it says," he said with narrowed eyes. "NOW!"

She laughed and waved the paper in the air. Each time he tried for it, she yanked it out of reach. Erin loved to tease her friend. His mouth would pucker up, and his eyes would turn to fire. The wrinkles on his forehead would crunch up like the tread on a car tire. And lately fun had been rare, because as a candidate, she had to be totally composed, just like the Queen of England. She had to be on guard every minute, using her best manners, never showing any disappointment, always smiling no matter what. One of the hardest things about being a candidate was putting your best foot forward *all* the time.

At school, she was dying to draw little red horns on Billy's poster and accidentally step on his pencils. She entertained the idea of hiding his homework so she could watch him panic when a 0 went up on the homework chart. Then she sighed. Erin Olson, the candidate, was tired of being perfect.

She stopped and looked seriously at her friend. "First off, the letters are of different sizes and colors, so they must have come from different sources. The edges are ragged, so I think the person was a boy, because there are more boys who don't care about neatness than girls . . . but then again, it could have been a sloppy girl," she said flashing him a quick grin.

He held his hand out but she pulled the letter closer to her body. Temple tapped his foot impatiently on the ground. Underneath his wire-framed glasses were two tiny slits eyeing her with his "I mean business" look.

She giggled. "Okay, okay . . . it says, 'Meet me at McDonalds. Purchase the two-for-one Big Mac special. Order the large fry. Sit at the table between Ronald McDonald and the exit sign. And bring plenty of ketchup.'"

"What?" he exclaimed. "That's not a message, that's a dinner date. Give it to me. I want to see for myself."

He rushed forward, trying to grab the paper from her hands. Erin grinned with delight and pushed him away. Then she tucked the paper behind her back. Before she realized it and could react, he pulled her forward with both hands and wrapped one arm around her in a headlock. They swayed back and forth as she tried to break free. She tripped him with her foot, he fell over sideways pulling her down, and the paper broke free and floated through the air. She leaped into the air and caught the paper with both hands, stuffing it quickly into her pocket. Temple tickled her middle, and she screamed in agony. Finally, his hands went up in surrender. She couldn't help but laugh.

"I give up, Rin. Since you're not going to tell me what it says, I'm going home." He stomped toward the front door with loud, pounding thumps.

"Temple . . . " She unfolded the crumpled paper. "Why are you so interested in this mystery?"

He turned back. "What do you mean?" he asked suspiciously.

"Why do you want to know what it says?" she asked. A small smile crossed her lips.

"Because you're my friend, and I care what happens to you. I know you don't want to take on Billy Perez by yourself. You need me." He turned his sad, droopy-eyed look on her.

Erin chuckled quietly to herself. This was the Temple she knew— an actor good enough for Broadway. When he was younger, he had totally fooled his mother with his pretending. He had stood on top of a hill in the middle of a field, sobbing like something was terribly wrong. Large crocodile tears had run down his face as he whimpered in terrible pain. He was so convincing, his mother had driven her car off the road, past a barricade, and into the meadow to rescue him. When she got there, he broke into a grin. His mother had not been pleased.

Erin giggled to herself, shaking her head back and forth. Even now, there were times when she couldn't tell if he was acting, but she knew the droopy-eyed puppy-dog look. That look was her favorite. When he turned his head and looked at her sideways, she couldn't say no. She pushed the paper toward him.

"'Go to General Taylor's statue at the end of the long walk,'" he read out loud. "Never heard of it."

"You know," she said. "The large statue in the park. You walk through the first park and take the footpath through the woods, along the river and into the next park. The trail ends at the top of the hill . . . it's probably about a five-mile walk. Grandpa and I did it last summer. The general and his horse sit at the very top of the last hill."

"Oh yeah, the statue of the general. The one who fought in the war," he said slowly. "The one with the huge bird's nest on top of his hat."

"I think I'll ask Grandpa to come along when we go," she said, thinking aloud. "He loves the general and the walk. And more important, he can keep an eye out for Billy."

"You mean you've told your grandfather about Billy and the clues?" replied Temple. "I thought we agreed not to tell anyone. I've kept my end of the bargain."

"I haven't told him yet," she said defensively. "I can't see any harm in him knowing. He doesn't have anything to do with the campaign, and he won't interfere, except if I'm in danger."

"But, Rinny, that's just it. Don't you think he'll be upset when he hears about the cemetery and the mine? And what do you think he's going to say about Miss Haggerty and the dungeon?" he pointed out anxiously. "The police would call that assault and battery."

A large black-and-blue bruise covered Erin's shin. Temple was right and she knew it. Things had become dangerous, and the clues were continuing. But now she knew Billy was following them for sure. Winston had seen Billy at the mansion, even though Temple thought it was a neighborhood boy. And she saw Billy wearing a ski mask at her kitchen window. Of course, Temple thought she was imagining things. And General Taylor's statue was out in an open area, where she would be able to see someone coming. This was the one clue where she had the advantage. Now was not a time to change things.

Temple placed the note flat on the table and pored over the message. After a thorough examination, he commented on the color pink clashing with the different colors of the letters. "Pink looks hideous with red and orange," he stated in his best professor voice.

The chalkboard, hanging next to the kitchen door, suddenly attracted Erin's attention. A message was scribbled across the center. The board was usually the first thing she checked after coming home, but tonight she had been distracted. She read the message twice.

"Look, Temple. I'm scheduled to give an interview in school tomorrow, with Channel 4 News. The school superintendent and his staff will be there, along with television cameras and reporters. Billy and I are going to be the leading human-interest story, showing at 6 p.m.," she said timidly. "Mrs. Brambles called to tell us so we could prepare for tomorrow."

"That's great, Rinny. You need the exposure. Up until now, only

Billy has made the news. Want me to help? We could write a speech together on the dangers of eating Tootsie Pops. We could say they wreck your nervous system and rot your teeth." He laughed and tried tickling her sides.

She pushed him away. "Temple, you have to leave right now."

"But why," he asked. "I'll help you write a speech. It'll be a great speech—trust me."

"Because," she said in a hurry, "I'm not worried about a stupid speech. I'm going to be on television and I don't have anything to wear ... and my hair! Look at me after being out in the rain! Go home Temple—I have to get ready for tomorrow." And before he could say another word, she pushed him out the door.

As she paced around the kitchen, Erin knew there wasn't time to worry about statues and horses and clues. Those things could wait. She had to prepare for an interview with the press. And tomorrow wasn't a day for worn out jeans and tennis shoes. Talking to the press meant she needed to look like a leader. She needed to look like someone who was brave. She needed to look like a real professional—and she had no idea what that look was.

TWENTY

THE REPORTER WITH THE ALLIGATOR SNOUT

The desk next to Erin's had been empty for some time now. Charlotte Pillman had been absent from school for over a week. There had been no nasty looks, no laser-beam stares, no jerking of Erin's chair. That also meant Charlotte wouldn't be there to make faces while she was talking to the television reporter. The inside of Charlotte's desk was a messy collection of papers and books. A broken crayon teetered at the edge of the opening, and wadded pieces of paper hid under an old crumpled lunch bag. Squeezed into the corner was a twisted paperback book bent like the letter "S."

Erin placed her homework neatly on top of her own desk. The morning bell would be ringing any second. Since she had walked into the classroom this morning, things had been chaotic. The boys were kicking and punching each other with karate moves. The girls were combing each other's hair into French braids and arguing over new shoes. The hamster had escaped from his cage, and three boys were sprawled out on the floor trying to trap him. One boy's ripe orange had been smashed on the bus and was now oozing inside his backpack. The paper monitor had dropped yesterday's homework assignments on the floor, scattering them everywhere. And of all days, the school custodian hadn't cleaned the room the night before. The trash cans were overflowing with yesterday's garbage. In a state of frantic nervous tension, Mrs. Brambles clapped her hands, and the noise stopped.

Billy Perez walked in, sporting a brilliant red tie over his bright white shirt. After pulling his new blue sports jacket into place, he combed his neatly trimmed hair. The children were in total awe. The girls smiled shyly, and the boys hooted and whistled. Billy bent over in a deep bow.

Erin looked down at her new hot pink tracksuit with the lavender stripe running across the front. The bright white leather tennis shoes still looked new, but she had polished them just in case. The hot pink headband matched the outfit perfectly. Yesterday in art class, she had drawn an alien face across her hand with permanent marker, not realizing she would be on television today. Her fingertips were sparkling clean, because she had practically scrubbed the skin off. She glanced quickly at Billy in his suit and then at her own outfit. Now she was really confused.

Billy walked past her desk on his way to the back. "Who's coming today? Shaquille O'Neal?" he said, reaching down to flick a speck off his perfectly polished shoes.

She gave him a small smile, trying to act unconcerned. He winked and hurried away. Billy raised his hands in high-five fashion as he approached the back of the room. Each boy slapped hard against his opened hand. He slid boldly into his chair and sat up straight. He motioned for his boys to do the same thing.

Mrs. Brambles went on to explain how Channel 4, the cable news station, would be interviewing the candidates. She gave hurried instructions, and the class moved quickly to clean the room. The class messenger had returned with two large trash bags, and the class fell to their knees, picking up trash and straightening desks. The attendance monitor recorded the roll. Mr. Cohen, the principal, took a seat at the back of the room next to the boys. Billy stood to welcome the principal and shake his hand.

A man dressed in jeans and a sweatshirt carried a bulky television camera into the room. A person with lights followed. The class grew silent. Down the hall, came the sharp sound of rapidly clicking heels. Several moments later, a woman wearing a bright red business suit marched through the doorway.

Mrs. Brambles pointed to the candidates. Erin moved sheepishly to the front blackboard. Billy pushed his way noisily past the desks in the back row and took a place next to her. Standing with his back perfectly straight, he smiled at the class, cleared his throat, and then folded his hands calmly in front of him. Erin copied his every move. Mrs. Brambles nodded, gave both of them a squeeze on the hand, then made her way to the back of the room. The students sat quietly.

"Excuse me," said the woman in the bright red suit. She turned toward Billy. "Where is the other candidate?"

"That's me, Miss Chan," replied Erin. The woman's name had been printed in large letters on her reporter's identification tag.

With lifted eyebrow, the woman skimmed Erin slowly from head to foot. Her eyes paused at the pink headband, and then followed the lavender stripe across the middle of the matching tracksuit. She stared momentarily at the clean white tennis shoes. Erin didn't breathe. She was afraid to move. The woman's eyes bore down on her like a laser beam scanning an enemy ship for weapons.

The reporter gave her a sharp look and then turned away with a frown. Erin felt the blood suddenly rush to her face as she turned a bright shade of red. The woman didn't like her. She turned toward Mrs. Brambles wondering what to do, but the teacher was whispering to the principal. Erin's heart sank.

She reviewed things several times to herself. The reporter would ask their names and grade and their reasons for wanting to be president. Then she would probably ask a human-interest question, like what are their hobbies and do they have any pets. And Erin was sure the reporter would ask about brothers and sisters.

The camera light went on, and the reporter turned on a smile. After talking engagingly into the camera, Miss Chan reached out to the candidates with her microphone. The logo, *Channel 4 News,* was impressed across the tip. The large silver dome hovered first under Miss Chan's lips and then directly under Billy's.

"Hello, this is Nancy Chan with Channel 4 News. Today, we are visiting Franklin Elementary, where a fifth-grade class is living through the rigors of democracy by staging its own presidential race. I am told by Mrs. Brambles, the teacher, that the two students running for office are doing an excellent job. Dedicated totally to the welfare of the fifth-grade class, they have been giving speeches, designing posters and explaining what they plan to do if elected. Today, we are here to get the inside scoop on our future politicians."

The reporter paused. Only the shuffling of the camera crew could be heard.

"Billy Perez," the reporter said sweetly, "I understand you have a long history of being a practical joker. Until this campaign, you were known to do such things as sprinkling pepper in your classmates' lunch milk and pouring pencil shavings into snow boots. I understand from the teacher that you have taken this lesson more seriously—something you haven't always done in the past. You have been the first person to volunteer for special projects and your schoolwork has been excellent—in fact, your behavior had improved tremendously. You, Billy Perez have become a role model. Can you explain this turnaround to the listeners and your fellow students?"

Erin looked awkwardly at Mrs. Brambles and then at the woman. She hadn't realized the reporter would ask questions like that. The teacher moved to the edge of her seat as if wanting to stand, and the troubled look that crossed Mrs. Brambles's face didn't make Erin feel any better. The principal crossed his arms. The school superintendent walked quietly into the room and stood beside the camera. Feeling suddenly more nervous than she had felt before, Erin hoped Billy would come up with an extraordinary answer. Everyone waited. But Billy Perez was silent.

Billy's face had turned chalky white. His startled eyes darted around the room. His lips twitched at first, then started to quiver. The television camera zoomed in for a closer shot. Billy stared at the camera. The camera zoomed in even closer. Billy's eyes were glued to the center. His quivering lips parted, but only a tiny grunt came out. The camera moved in and out, with Billy's face growing larger and then smaller on the television screen.

The spotlights gave off an intense heat. The reporter lifted the microphone to his nose. His eyes broke free of the camera and darted back and forth across the room again. Erin watched Billy shrink into a speechless, tiny ball.

Erin bit her lower lip. This was not the kid who had poured a bottle of dish detergent into the school water fountain. This was not the kid who had collected one hundred signatures to protest the use of in-house detentions. This was not the Billy she knew.

A small drop of perspiration trickled down his face. Billy's shaky hands rattled against the loose change in his pocket. He swallowed. Tears welled up in his eyes. Erin knew the class couldn't see the teary rims of his eyes, and she was thankful. Billy Perez was in terrible trouble.

The King of the Clowns was scared stiff.

"Billy, what do you think are the duties of a class president?" asked the reporter, in a thundering voice.

His eyes fixed again on the camera lens. Another trickle of perspiration ran down his cheek.

"How do you feel about competing against a girl?" she continued. "Do you feel girls can make good presidents? Are they tough enough to make the hard decisions? Would you select a girl for vice president? Do you have any girls for friends?"

Feeling very uneasy, Erin drew in a deep breath. This interview wasn't what she had expected at all. Where were the questions about brothers and sisters and favorite classes . . . or whether or not they liked their teachers? Where were the questions about the actual campaign?

"I understand, Billy, that you can be an 'A' student when you want to be—and that you have been expelled from another school for mischievous behavior. What makes you think you should be a class president?" asked the woman harshly.

Erin gasped with the rest of the class. *Billy Perez had been expelled from another school?* The reporter's eyes sparkled. A contemptuous smile crept across her lips. Billy stared straight ahead without moving. Erin shuffled uncomfortably by his side.

"Mrs. Brambles," snapped the reporter impatiently, "I understood these children were to be prepared. What is wrong with them?"

Erin nudged Billy with her shoulder. His trembling hand reached for hers. The boys in the back of the classroom snickered. The superintendent looked appalled. Mrs. Brambles stood up to speak but before she could say anything Erin stepped before the camera.

"Billy Perez deserves to be class president because he has been doing the best job he knows how to do," she said boldly, patting him firmly on the back. "He is a worthy opponent and would make a fine leader. He has run an excellent campaign. You see that poster, over there? The poster that says, 'Billy Perez cares.' That was his idea. He wanted all his classmates to know this campaign was about them. It is not about competition between boys and girls. We are bigger than that, Miss Chan."

Erin held her shoulders back and looked directly into the reporter's eyes. Mrs. Brambles and the principal clapped. The television camera zoomed in for a close up. The reporter inched in closer, and Erin could feel the woman's breath against her face.

"So, Erin, you feel Billy should be president instead of you?" asked the woman abruptly.

"I think," said Erin, a little more cautiously, "both Billy and I would make good presidents."

"Even though you've claimed he attacked you? I understand you have also accused him of stalking you." The reporter quickly gestured for the camera to turn toward the audience.

Erin drew back in horror and glanced across the classroom. What person had told the reporter she had accused Billy of stalking her? She had apologized, and Billy had accepted. That wasn't news—that was gossip! The students were staring at her. She combed each face, searching for a guilty sign. The principal looked away, and the boys in the back of the room made pig faces. The lights from the television camera blinded her. The reporter faded behind the strange, flashing lights.

Drawing in another deep breath, she found her voice turning into a squeak. "My grandfather says a good leader should check all the facts before speaking."

"But, that's not what you did, Erin Olson. You blatantly accused Billy Perez of attacking you, didn't you?" hissed the woman.

Erin blinked. The woman's mouth was growing four long fangs. Each fang took the shape of a sharpened dagger. Then the face surrounding the fangs stretched out like a balloon, into the elongated snout of an alligator. The eyes above the snout turned into black slits. The slits twirled against the bright yellow background, like cats-eye marbles spinning on the ground. That's when Erin felt herself starting to shrink. She was growing smaller and smaller as the eyes spun faster and faster. She was slipping slowly away, going down, down, down, as her once-tall frame became miniature. Down into her shoes she fell, the slick sides of white leather engulfing her tiny little body. She tumbled deep into the vast, dark void of a gigantic toe. Voices echoed in the distance as she struggled to stand.

"Didn't you, Erin Olson?" repeated the reporter.

Erin could hear the voice drifting in a far-away world. She struggled to answer. She cleared her voice and blinked. Suddenly she was no longer lost inside her shoes. She was fully-grown and standing under the nose of the *Channel 4 News* camera. The twirling eyes stopped, and the reporter's face snapped back into shape. Erin glanced at Billy Perez. He was still staring straight ahead. She straightened her top, put on her best smile and looked once again into the camera.

"My name is Erin Olson," she began. "And I would like to tell you about our school project on democracy. We are learning how the political process works by staging our own presidential campaign. Two candidates were chosen to run, Billy Perez and myself. I would like the students to vote for me, because I have many ideas for improving our fifth-grade class. I want the class, as a team, to work together on recycling and helping to improve the neighborhood. Thank you. Oh yeah, I also have a cat named Teddy."

Erin ignored the squinty looks from the reporter. Mrs. Brambles had sat down again, and was looking very pleased. One of the crew gave her a thumb's up from behind Miss Chan's back.

She leaned into the camera and held Billy's hand up. "This is Billy Perez, the other candidate running for president. I don't know if he has any pets, but he does have a sister. Emily is in third grade. He wants to be president because he feels he could be a good leader also. Oh, and thank you, again."

She walked Billy back to his seat before dropping into her own. The reporter marched out of the room, her heels again making the rapid clickety-clak sound as she strode down the hallway. The television crew followed her out the door, with the camera and lights in tow. Erin stared at the notebook sitting on her desktop. The pen with the four different colors begged to be picked up. After clicking on the color green, she drew two green circles inside the "o's," in the word "notebook." Next came the red ink, for the long hairy eyebrows above the perfectly round eyes. Mrs. Brambles had begun the math lesson.

TWENTY-ONE

9eNeRƏL TƏYLOR

"Rinny, I saw Billy talking to a group of students at lunch," Temple said, as he walked briskly down the dirt trail. The five-mile path to General Taylor's statue wound along the river, through the woods and into a clearing. "He says he learned a big lesson from the interview with Channel 4 News. He said just because something looks easy, doesn't mean it is. He told everyone how he couldn't wait to talk to the reporter until he looked into the camera and realized there were thousands of faces watching his every move on the other side."

Erin and Temple walked at a fast pace. Birds chirped in the nearby trees. Erin had been quiet, hoping Temple wouldn't say anything to spoil the day. The flowing river gurgled next to them.

"And he said he will remember that when he's president. He will remember that sometimes people get into trouble and need help . . . and as president he will never forget what other people go through. Then he quoted the old Indian saying, 'Never judge a person until you have walked a mile in their moccasins.'"

Erin didn't look up. Her eyes followed the ground as they passed into the thick woods. Somehow, she knew the whole interview mess would turn out to help Billy. He had proven to be a master of spin . . . turning something bad into something good. The image of the reporter's face was still fresh in her mind. She only wanted to forget about it.

"I think he was smart to admit he was scared," continued Temple. "Now the students feel sorry for him. He's no longer just a clown, but a real person with feelings."

"I knew you were going to say something like that," Erin said, feeling suddenly glum. "I felt sorry for him, myself. He has most of the boys' votes already, just because he's Billy. Now, some of the girls will vote for him, too."

"That is a problem, my dear," said Temple thoughtfully. "How about calling the reporter and scheduling another interview? This time, don't be brave . . . tremble and shake . . . weep . . . tell her how you've always been misunderstood—anything to drum up sympathy. Give it your best."

Erin giggled at the thought. "I'm afraid Billy has already done that."

"Oh, and there was something else . . . " Temple paused, stepping over a fallen branch. "Bernard-the-weasel showed up. He had been sulking around the crowd listening to Billy speak. The minute he saw me, he started with the dirty looks. I saw one of your pink pencils sticking out of his shirt pocket . . . you know, the ones with your name imprinted across the top in a smile. He hid it inside a trouser pocket as soon as he saw me."

Erin hopped over a pit in the path. "I thought Charlotte Pillman took that pencil. I guess I'll have to take my pencils to school one at a time and keep track of them."

"I gave him the business," chuckled Temple. "He tripped over his own feet trying to get away from me. It's a good thing I'm around, or he might show up on your doorstep like a sick puppy dog."

Erin tried to imagine poor Bernard-the-weasel, standing on her doorstep, all hunched over with a handful of flowers . . . only the flowers would be crushed, because Bernard had fallen on them on his way over . . . and the box of chocolates tucked under his arm would be empty. On the front of his shirt would be smeared chocolate stains, evidence of a snack on his trip over. Then he would stand there on the porch, shifting nervously from one foot to the other. Even if he didn't eat the chocolates, he would stand there looking guilty of something he didn't do. But worst of all, Erin couldn't count on Bernard's vote, because he was in a different fifth-grade class.

Broken twigs and gravel covered the ground. Erin hustled to keep up with Temple's long legs. She was fast, but not as fast as the town's first-place track star. Grandfather hadn't been invited, leaving the two of them to examine the general by themselves—the two of them and Billy. She knew Billy would follow just so he could watch them hunt for the clue. Her skin was tingling. He was close by.

They stopped at a picnic table and ate the snack she had brought. Inside the paper bag were two bottled waters, fat pretzels with plenty of salt, cheese sticks and homemade brownies, compliments of her grandfather's tin. There wasn't any evidence of the strawberries she had eaten while Temple wasn't looking.

The hiking trail ended at the top of a hill. Woods surrounded the clearing and lined the far side of the river that ran alongside the trail. General Taylor's long, sharp nose pointed toward the ground. In his right hand, was a sword raised toward the heavens. A Sharp's single-shot rifle lay across the saddle. The enormous iron horse reared back on two muscular legs, permanently poised for the charge. Nestled inside the shallow top of the general's army hat were the shattered remains of a large bird's nest. A six-foot cement pedestal supported the structure underneath.

They stood at the base and looked up. It was as tall as a two-story house. Erin was too short to climb on top of the pedestal. Temple bent over, cupped his hand and offered to hoist her up.

Erin lifted her foot.

"I'll look for the clue, Rinny, if you want me too. The general looks really difficult to climb and, if I were you, I wouldn't mess with him. Did you catch the look on his face?" Temple leaned against the cement wall for support.

The general's dark, intense eyes targeted an invisible mark. Unbreakable, willful determination defined the sculpted lines of his face.

"Don't worry; I'll be all right. This statue can't be any harder than the cherry tree in my back yard," she replied. Temple pushed her up from underneath until she crawled onto the base of the pedestal. "Besides, as a candidate it's important I find the clues," she said, teasingly.

She scooted slowly around the base of the statue, holding onto the slippery surface. The horse was gigantic. Its long flowing tail hung down next to its hind legs, pointing toward the cement base. Even on tiptoe, Erin's fingers barely touched the knobby knees of the stallion. The metal surface had peaks and valleys, but nowhere to hold. If she climbed up the tail she might be able to reach the saddle.

The tail's fine, hair-like grooves were thin enough for a hand to grasp. She grabbed the tail and pulled up, her feet pushing at the same time. Grunting with every tug, she moved slowly up the rump. That slippery surface was hard to maneuver. It took several attempts before she could find a place to grip. She pulled with all her might. Her excitement mounted as she rose to the top. Then all of a sudden, her right foot slipped and she fell, going down, down, down, all the way to the pedestal. Her bottom hit with a thump.

Temple cried out in terror. "Rinny! Are you all right? Talk to me girl!" He paced the area anxiously, never taking his eyes off of her.

Erin untwisted herself and stood. A quick tug pulled her clothes into place. She looked at the horses tail, grabbed hold of it and shinnied up like a professional. She pulled one hand up over the other, finally rolling onto the wide backside of the horse.

Temple jumped for joy. She leaned toward him and bowed. Then she turned outward. Her heart quickened at what she saw next. At the base of the slope on which the statue stood, was the river, with its swiftly moving rapids. One tiny slip could send her headfirst into the turbulent water. Closing her eyes, she willed herself not to think about it.

A soft breeze blew against her face, and she opened her eyes to a breathtaking view. "Oh, Temple it's beautiful up here. I can see the entire path of the river, snaking its way along the woods. I can see parts of the town, I can see the church on West Street . . . and I can see the Court House. I can see little tiny football players in the park . . . and I see . . . I see a boy watching us from over there!" she screamed hysterically. "It's Billy, Temple! Get him!"

Temple whirled around and broke into a full sprint. He zigzagged back and forth aiming for the spot where Billy had been spotted.

"He darted in between those two large pine trees," she screamed, pointing to a clearing straight ahead.

A mysterious figure darted into the thickest part of the woods. Her eyes followed the small shape until the dense foliage covered the view. Temple disappeared into the opening behind him. Erin wanted to jump off the horse and help, but she stopped after leaning over the edge. Everything on the ground looked so small. The dirt path leading up to the statue was now a little strand of spaghetti. The land between the river and the general seemed to disappear altogether. The way to the bottom was a long, hard drop. For some reason, it seemed much further down than up, and there wasn't anything to keep her from tumbling into the water. She chewed on her bottom lip and decided to wait patiently for her friend to return.

A large black crow circled above, shattering the peace with its shrill screech. Her heart pounded, the minutes dragging slowly by. Now she would become president. Billy was caught at his own game. But, she wouldn't call Miss Chan at Channel 4 News and report the dirty details. And she wouldn't brag about it to the newspaper, either. A public resignation wasn't necessary. She would let Billy withdraw from the campaign like a gentleman.

The branches to the opening moved, and she held her breath. A figure emerged. Temple walked out of the woods into the clearing, alone. Holding up two empty hands, he shook his head back and forth. Her shoulder's sagged as her head dropped in agony.

"It was someone else, Rin," he called out. "He was just a boy who lives close by. We scared him away from his fishing hole when we arrived. He wanted to know what we were doing, that's all. I told him to go home. See, Billy wasn't following us . . . your imagination is running wild again, My Lady."

Erin buried her head in her hands and moaned. Something had gone wrong. Temple didn't catch the right boy. Billy Perez was here, and she knew it. He had managed to get away at the last second. Billy Perez had triumphed again.

Temple climbed up effortlessly onto the base of the statue and faced Erin overhead. "Did you find a clue?" he asked.

"Not yet," she answered, sadly. She looked around the park once more, before returning to the search. Billy Perez would have to wait. Again.

A gentle breeze blew across the water, pushing her ponytail high in the air. The endless rapid waters below tumbled furiously downstream. The climb across the saddle to the general's lap was dangerous. Only the narrow rim provided a place for her feet. She edged across on tiptoe, her hands grasping at the folds in the general's uniform. The rim suddenly became thinner toward the front of the saddle. Her foot slipped, but the rifle's tip was just within reach. She clung to it with both hands. Her heart thumped as she searched the rim with her foot. After finding what she was looking for, she planted both feet on a firmer foothold.

With a hand holding fast to the rifle, she leaned out to inspect the area. There wasn't anything unusual inside the twisted surface of the iron overcoat, and the tip of the rifle barrel was welded shut. Every ledge was empty. The rounded lap held only the general's famous buffalo rifle.

"See anything?" called Temple.

"Nothing. There isn't any place to hide a clue. I need to climb on top of the head and shoulders."

"Don't you dare!" Temple cried. Before uttering another word, he shinnied up the horse's tail. "It's far more dangerous than it looks, and penny loafers aren't good for climbing."

Erin glanced at the black penny loafers with the shiny pennies on top. How could he say that? She had climbed the cherry tree and old man's cave in her favorite shoes. They were tight on her feet when she first bought them, but after a while, they had broken into the perfect size, flopping up and down nicely when she walked.

"You almost fell, Rin. You need shoes with rubber soles for climbing. That's why we wear rubber-soled shoes in P.E. . . . for traction." He pulled his shoelaces tight.

"Oh, okay," she said, working her way slowly back to where he stood. "But, I wanted to be the one to find this clue. I'll only agree to it if I get to examine it first."

"Of course," he said, before hoisting himself effortlessly up to the general's shoulders like Spiderman. Wrapping his arms around the general's neck, he searched the folds in the metal jacket, and then swung around to the front sleeve. He stood like a sailor with his hands above his eyes, looking out across the land. "I don't see Billy," he said teasingly. Then he climbed up the right arm to look inside the hat.

Watching with amazement, Erin gasped with every move. Temple was a good athlete, but she never knew he could climb like this. He attacked the statue like it was a playground jungle gym—up and over, down and under, swaying recklessly by the arms. She squeezed her eyes shut several times, but opened them again when she didn't hear a thud.

"Rin, I wish you could see this," he called out. "There's a pink egg inside the nest. It's one of those plastic eggs used for Easter. I'm going to bring it down." With that, he placed the oblong object inside his jacket and slid down the horse's tail to the cement base where Erin waited.

She held her hand out.

A glint sparkled in Temple's eyes. "It's only fair that *I* study the egg before letting it leave my person," he declared.

His arms folded and rested over the bulge inside his jacket. Erin didn't move at first; then her eyebrows puckered in confusion. She held her hand out again. He stepped back and snickered.

"You aren't still mad because there were nuts in your brownie are you?" Her mind raced with possible explanations for his behavior. She couldn't help it if only one corner of the brownie didn't have pecans and she was forced to eat the bigger piece. It wasn't her fault he didn't like nuts. As a matter of fact, she wouldn't have shared it at all if she'd known he was going to be so grouchy about it. Now, even though he'd eaten the rest of the food she'd brought, he was taking his disappointment over the brownie out on her when she wanted the clue.

"Temple," she objected, "you promised. This is my mystery, and that means the egg is meant for me." She waved her open hand again under his nose.

"Correction . . . I didn't promise. And why should I give it to you? So you can tease me like before? I don't think so. If you want it, you'll just have to take it away."

With one leap he took off for the woods.

TWENTY-TWO

The Sucking Swamp

Erin looked at the sharp drop down to the ground. There was no easy way to get off of General Taylor's statue, and there was no time to worry about being hurt. Temple had the clue, and the only way to get it back was to follow him into the woods.

"Temple! Stop!" she shouted. Then she jumped to the ground with a bold leap. A sharp pain shot up through her legs. Temple disappeared through the opening. She hobbled slowly across the meadow, and followed him through the pine trees and into the woods.

Dry pine needles crunched underfoot as she made her way through the dense trees. There was no sight of Temple and the pink egg. Temple was gone. She hesitated to go any further. This was a strange and eerie part of the woods where, it was rumored, ghosts and goblins lived. Last Halloween, someone saw the head of General Taylor floating through the air. And during a thunderstorm the next day, his headless body had ridden into town and scared Mr. Smith to death. Even her grandfather repeated the story of the bank robber who had hidden in the woods and never came out again. It was told how the bank's sack full of money was discovered, untouched, years later in a den full of man-sized spider webs. The very thought gave her goose bumps.

Under the towering pine trees lay a carpet of brown needles, stretching as far as the eye could see. The lowest tree branch hovered well above the head of the tallest man in town. Small saplings of underbrush tried sprouting along the sun-starved ground. The temperature was ten degrees cooler inside the woods.

Erin buttoned her jacket with a shiver, trying to remember that rumors were only stories—at least she hoped so—and there was a trail to follow.

Pushing the scary thoughts from her mind, she began to search until she found a tiny pine tree flattened against the ground. Something heavy had passed this way. A closer look revealed a bare spot in the pine needles . . . a bare spot made by a passing shoe. Similar marks followed the riverbank and then stopped at a swampy area where the low ground gathered water from the forest when it rains. Standing water, mixed with broken branches, leaves and needles, turned into a thick, gooey mud. She looked beyond the blocked path and noticed the top of a decomposed tree trunk just above the gooey surface.

The swamp was too wide for jumping, and thorny brush covered both ends. Picking up a nearby branch, she poked the top of the tree trunk. The rotten wood crumbled underneath. The fallen tree branches were too thin for building a bridge, and the tree trunk was too rotten to use it as a stepping-stone. Walking backwards, she rechecked the trail. The path did, indeed, lead up to this point.

There was no other choice—cross or head back.

Erin noticed a fallen tree on the other side. Water and mud covered the underside, and lying on the ground not far from the tree was something pink among the browns and greens of the forest floor. She moved to get a closer look. It was the pink egg . . . the pink egg once tucked inside Temple's coat!

"Temple!" she called out hopefully. "Temple! Where are you?"

Complete silence filled the air. A whirlwind of leaves blew across her feet. A squirrel scampered over the rotten tree trunk, across the fallen tree, and onto the other side. She called out again, her voice dropping off to a whisper. The bright color of the plastic egg stuck out among the soft earth tones. If Temple had dropped it, he would return.

Poking the bottom of the swamp with a stick, she discovered it was only eight or nine inches deep. Unfortunately, each time she pushed the stick into the mud, a sucking sound came out, and the stick stood in place. The sucking swamp was a gigantic magnet.

The forest ground was littered with leaves and twigs. Erin kicked the leaves into the swamp—pinecones, needles and twigs flew through the air. Her jacket became a basket, cradling all the branches and leaves she could find. She ran back and forth between the swamp and the cluttered ground, piling jacket-ful after jacket-ful into the water. Every time she smacked the leaves down with a branch, a great sucking noise pulled the leaves under. Determined to get to the egg first, she worked faster and faster. Finally, the dam was built.

A nice dry path of leaves stretched across the swamp to the other side. A rustling noise disturbed the quiet on the other side of the swamp. Temple came running back for the egg, his eyes fixed on the pink shape like an Olympic runner going for the prize. Startled, Erin looked nervously at the dam. The egg was on the other side of the swamp, and Temple was getting closer . . . and within the egg was the next clue. She had to get to the egg before him.

Jumping onto her man-made bridge, she moved forward. Halfway across the crunchy path, her feet started to sink. She paused. The water began to seep in around her shoes. She looked up. Temple was flying through the air. The pink egg glistened on the other side. She broke into a run, one step, two steps, three steps. She could feel herself getting closer to the bank. Suddenly her feet went under. The great sucking noise pulled her down, down, down. The thick gooey mud slid into her shoes, in between her toes, and up to her ankles. She tried to lift her feet, but the more she struggled, the further she sank.

Temple suddenly stopped and turned around. Erin didn't wait for him to move again. She pulled on her right leg with both hands. Her foot broke free, but the shoe was buried beneath the mud. Stepping onto a thicker part of the bridge, she pulled on her left foot. The left shoe stayed beneath the mud, too. She stood shoeless in knee-deep slime. Struggling to lift one leg after the other, she moved slowly toward the bank.

A puzzled expression covered Temple's face. He looked in her direction, and as if listening to something behind him, turned back the way he had come. Before retreating into the woods, he took a last glance at the egg, and then disappeared from sight.

The prickly pine cones bit into Erin's feet as she slogged through the goop. The heavy, wet mud soaked up by her pant legs made the struggle worse. She reached the egg and flopped down. An icy sensation swept across her feet and deep into her toes. Both feet were caked in brown mud and covered with a thick layer of dried pine needles. The mud-drenched socks stared back at her like two prickly porcupines.

Sighing, she placed the egg inside her pocket, which she promptly zipped shut. Sucking noise or not, she wasn't going any further until her loafers were fished out of the swamp.

TWENTY-THREE

The Strange Message

Erin knelt beside the riverbank and leaned over the lapping water to rinse the mud from her socks and black penny loafers. Needles and dirt washed away in a waterfall of brown liquid. Over and over again, she dipped her shoes, thinking of the pioneers walking west. They had learned in school that drowning was one of the four most common causes of death. Her eyes locked onto the unstoppable current. The rushing water beat repeatedly against the bank, spraying cold droplets of water against her face. The water tumbled, over and over again, never stopping, never caring.

After she rinsed the mud from her socks, she squeezed until the last drop of water fell from her fingertips. Just like the pioneers, she would return them to her bare feet and continue on. She placed her socks and shoes on the bank and stepped into the shallow water. The tumbling waters washed away the swampy film from her jeans. The ice-cold wash left her jeans surprisingly clean, as clumps of mud and debris tumbled downstream.

The afternoon sun was getting lower, and she needed to find Temple before the sun set. Once the sun was gone, she would be all alone and blind in the dark. In spite of that, she wanted one little peek at the next clue. Unzipping the pocket containing the egg, she removed her prize. There wasn't anything unusual about it. It was an ordinary plastic egg, used for candy during Easter. As she opened it, a tightly folded note popped out. It read:

H r l e t e a t l e a p B r h a t e h r h
e e i s h l s c u H p y i t d y h C u c

The letters didn't make any sense at all. They didn't fall into neat little groups like words. Reading the letters from right to left, instead of left to right, didn't work either. Putting the first five letters, "H r l e t," into a group didn't spell anything. Neither did groups of two, three or four. She held the paper upside down and tried doing a word search. The words, "eat, leap, let, it" didn't form any sentence she could understand. And there were too many possibilities, if you tried unscrambling them. Another idea came to her. If she went back one letter in the alphabet for every letter in the code, then she might uncover the true meaning. That meant "H" would be "G," "R" would be "Q," and "L" would be "K," etc . . . Squinting at the paper, she wrote the new letters in the mud. The new letters didn't form a sentence, either. It was just another jumbled mess of gibberish.

She thought and thought. Maybe these were coordinates on a map. But how, which map, and why? She sighed. Temple had studied secret codes and espionage. He, Billy Perez, Bernard-the-weasel, and most of the children from school had taken the secret writing class at the Science Museum, a class she had missed because she was grounded for eating the icing off Grandpa's cupcakes. Not just one cupcake, either. She was grounded for eating the icing off of all the cupcakes. For some reason, she couldn't help herself with the yummy cream-cheese flavor. And when Grandfather had offered their neighbor a snack from his tin, he discovered all ten cupcakes had been licked clean.

She made sure the egg was sealed shut and then pushed it inside her pocket. This was the pocket with no holes and a zipper. She wouldn't lose the egg like Temple had. There would be time to think about the message later. Time was too important to waste now. She had to get back and prepare for tomorrow.

Tomorrow was going to be a big day. Mrs. Brambles had scheduled the two candidates to speak before the entire school. Mr. Cohen had even invited all the children in the school to an assembly in the auditorium to hear the last speech before the vote—the vote her fifth-grade class would be casting afterwards. Unfortunately, there was still loads of work to do. She needed to call and personally tell each student her plans for a new student government. Even Charlotte Pillman was on the list.

She wrestled with the wet socks. The wet cotton material stretched across her foot like an elastic band. The line across the toe stretched to her heels. And the line across the heels stretched up to her shin, turning the once ankle socks into knee socks. Then, there was the problem of the wet shoes. Wet socks did not slide into wet leather. Desperately forcing the shoe by twisting back and forth didn't work either. Her toes slid in halfway and stopped. Her heels hung out, crushing the back rims of the loafers down to the ground. Her favorite penny loafers were now clogs. She whimpered. It was a five-mile walk back to the house.

She stood, as ready as she would ever be, in soaking wet jeans and socks and shoes that wore like clogs. As she walked, the shoes flopped up and down against her heels, flinging a gritty layer of leaves and needles in between her socks and shoes. Determination drove her to hunt for Temple so they could head for home. The sun would be starting to set any time, now, and there was important work to do.

A piercing scream erupted upstream.

TWENTY-FOUR

HELPLESS

The scream stopped, swallowed by the rapids. Erin turned to see an oncoming figure thrash wildly in the water. The person trapped inside the river was frantically fighting to keep his or her head above the rapidly moving current. The victim's face sent her reeling backwards in horror. It was her beloved friend, Temple.

She clumsily followed the current along the riverbank, her shoes flopping awkwardly up and down. The swift water was pushing Temple dangerously ahead. Tumbling helplessly out of control, his arms and legs surfaced over and over again. His head rose twice, his gaping mouth gasping for air. Her heart stopped each time he disappeared.

The river curved back on itself before reaching the falls. If she took the shortcut through the woods, she could get downstream just ahead of him. Maybe she would find a branch to throw into the water . . . a vine, or anything that he could hold on to. Or maybe the river would push him close to the bank so she could catch him.

She pulled her shoes off and, holding one in each hand, began running. Her wet socks crunched against the forest floor. Pinecones, twigs and rocks tortured her already troubled feet. She turned her mind away from the pain. Pushing harder and harder, she shot through the trees, her breaths coming in short, rapid bursts. The sharp pains reached deep inside her soul. A stream of tears fell, but she kept moving. She was a strong northern wind, weaving in and out of the cool autumn air. She was a wingless bird, soaring high above the ground. She dodged in and out, passing tree after tree. She jumped over walls of thornbush, scrambled down a valley, and clawed her way up the other side. She was tripped by creeping tree roots and tangled in a web of vines. Her lungs burned as they filled with air and her heart pounded like thunder. All she could think of was Temple and making it to the downstream riverbank in time.

The trees grew thinner, sunlight breaking through the once-dense branches. She burst out of the woods, eyeing the river just ahead. With one last push, she landed on the riverbank. A strong current gnashed against the rocks. Gasping for air, she dropped to her knees and panted. Both her sides ached. She clasped them and inhaled deeply, wheezing with every breath. It was a strain to see upstream. Temple wasn't in the water. Turning her head in the other direction allowed her a clear view of the path downstream. He wasn't anywhere to be seen. She had made it ahead of schedule.

Struggling to her feet, Erin searched the surroundings. The ground was bare, except for dry pine needles. There were no fallen trees, no vines, and no branches, nothing that could be used as a lifesaver. But further up the bank, and jutting out several feet over the water, was a thick, knotted root. The dirt around the twisted root had washed away with the river's current, leaving it exposed. It belonged to a mature, healthy tree well anchored in the forest ground. Erin jumped into the water and hung on.

Temple appeared around the bend, his arms helplessly thrashing in the water. He gasped for air but was pulled under. Erin pulled off her blue nylon windbreaker, the only thing she had. She twisted it around and around, the material becoming tighter with each turn, until it formed a straight line. She planned to wrap one sleeve around her wrist and throw the jacket across the water to Temple. It would unwrap in midair but possibly reach Temple before falling limp again. Then it would be up to Temple, and only if he saw her throw it in the first place.

Temple disappeared below the rapids again, the white foamy water churning under. Hooking her arm through the web-like tendrils of the farthest end of the root, Erin leaned into the waves. The rapids continued to pound, the waves turning over and over. She screamed, but the rushing waters overpowered her voice. Her heart stopped, and for the first time, she knew real terror.

Up until now, she had thought of Temple as invincible. But now the river was a powerful enemy, where strength and brains didn't matter. It was in control, and Temple was under its command. He had been down for too long. Erin didn't know what to do. Panic tried to paralyze her thoughts but a renewed energy cleared her mind. Jumping out into the rapids would be suicide and a dead person couldn't help. The river would have power over two victims instead. Maybe a bend further down the river would offer another chance. If only her friend could survive that long.

Suddenly, Temple popped straight up, his head rising high in the air. The waters whipped him around again. Taking a chance, Erin screamed and threw the jacket out. Temple disappeared below the churning waters. So did the jacket. A heaviness pulled the windbreaker out into the river.

Hooking on to the thick root with her left arm, Erin gripped the jacket in her other hand. She struggled with the immense weight pulling it away. The outstretched muscles of her arm ached as she grasped the slipping sleeve. Closing her eyes, she summoned all her strength, willing herself to hold on. No matter what happened, she couldn't let go.

The weight on the other end of the jacket pulled back and forth. The river's water plunged into the rocks, then pulled the current out again. Every time the water pushed in, the jacket followed, and her muscles felt a short-lived relief. Then the object would be pulled out, straining every muscle all over again.

Then, as if by magic, the weight became lighter. It no longer depended on the current. The task became easier, and she pulled back as far as she could. The jacket surfaced along the top of the water and moved slowly in toward the bank.

Erin, whose eyes had been glued to the water, now saw another hand on the jacket. She turned to see someone next to her, helping to pull the jacket in with both hands. Twisting around, she glanced directly into the face of Billy Perez. His blue eyes were focused on the river. His clenched teeth and taut muscles told of the immense weight he was bearing. He continued to pull, both hands wrapped tightly in place, as he backed toward the riverbank. Erin, too, pulled with all her strength.

Temple's head floated above the water, his hands clutching the jacket. The outgoing water pulled him away again. Billy dropped the jacket, reached out with both hands, and grabbed Temple's arms. Erin gripped the collar of Temple's jacket, and together they pulled him in. They rolled him onto the flat surface of the riverbank; his face ash white in color.

"Temple! You're safe! Wake up," Erin cried anxiously.

She placed her ear to his heart. There was no beat. She felt his wrist. There was no pulse. She rolled him over on his side, and water poured from his mouth. She placed him on his back, turning his head to one side. All the different lifesaving techniques taught in school raced through her mind. Placing her overlapped hands flat on his chest, she pushed down. Water poured from his lips, and the coughing began. Erin sat back on her heels wearily and cried.

Temple was alive.

TWENTY-FIVE

THE CLOWN SHOES

Temple's chest rose and fell with each breath. The water had been forced from his lungs, but he was trembling. Erin brushed the hair from his face and placed her hands gently on his arm. He was cold, and there wasn't anything to cover him with. He groaned unconsciously.

"Billy, help me, we need to pull him to higher ground," Erin said faintly. She was suddenly feeling exhausted, her arms and legs now wobbly. She expected Billy to reply as she tried warming Temple's arms by briskly rubbing the skin with her hands. It was important for the blood to return to his sickly white flesh. She picked up each hand and rubbed gently. Billy did not reply.

She looked up and quickly scanned the woods. Billy was nowhere to be seen. He had stepped forward when Temple's life depended on it, and she was grateful, but now he was gone. Temple's arms were totally limp as she rubbed gently.

Billy Perez had really surprised her. She remembered a visit to her class from a chemist, before the campaign began. As a plastics specialist, the chemist had explained how versatile plastics were in our lives. He had told how everyday items like vitamins were stored in plastic containers, then shrink-wrapped with plastic for safety and freshness. She remembered the smirk across Billy's face when he had raised his hand, and the look on the chemist's face, when Billy had asked if a dead person could be preserved with shrink-wrap. Of course, the class broke out in uncontrollable laughter. The new Billy wouldn't have asked such a question.

Since running for president, he had become a totally different person. He rarely visited the principal's office anymore, and he had even stopped drawing little faces on her posters. Yesterday afternoon, he had volunteered to help the first graders with reading. Little groups of first graders sat in the hallway with Billy's organized fifth-grade student teams.

The older students helped each first-grade reading group with phonics. Mr. Cohen, the principal, observed with pride.

Erin tried to pull Temple up the bank, but her arms collapsed like worn out rubber bands. A chill was creeping into her skin, accompanying the throbbing of her sore feet. Temple thrashed in his sleep, his arms swatting wildly in the air. Erin tried to hold them down. His muffled grunts and wincing scared her. Unconscious, Temple was reliving his trip down the river. That was when she noticed his left leg. It didn't move. The poor, twisted limb turned inward toward the other foot. Temple was hurt, and they were miles from the nearest help.

Sitting with her knees up, she buried her head inside her arms, desperately trying to think. The temperature would fall drastically and Temple was already shivering, thanks to the river's icy waters.

"Billy Perez! I need you!" she screamed. The new Billy did not respond. She screamed again as loud as she could. Nothing. She screamed in a different direction. Nothing again. It would be risky to leave Temple alone on the ground in the woods, but there was no other choice. She had to find help. The boy who had spied on them at the statue probably lived nearby. And where there were people, there would be telephones.

A patch of oak trees grew along the riverbank, their curly leaves gathering like a blanket across the ground. Her grandfather had said paper was made from wood, and paper was good insulation. Oak leaves were from trees, and her grandfather used the curly leaves to protect the bushes in the winter by piling them around the base of each bush. Maybe leaves could offer warmth and protection to Temple, too.

Using her foot like a broom, Erin swept the leaves across the ground, covering Temple's body. She was careful not to kick up the dirt. The mound of leaves grew higher and higher. Her goal was to cover his entire body in a foot of leaves but let his head remain exposed. She didn't want him to be frightened when he awoke, and she didn't want to lose sight of him either. If she could see his head, then she knew she could find him again. And, just to make sure, she draped her wet jacket, which she knew would do her no good even though she had wrung it out as much as she could, over the pile of leaves. The heat of exercise would keep her warm better than a wet jacket.

Her loafers lay next to her on the ground. With everything that had happened, she had forgotten about her sore feet and smashed shoes. But standing there in mud-coated, stretched-out socks brought the problem back to her. She brushed the leaves away from Temple's feet and examined his shoes.

He had a passion for the old-fashioned Converse basketball shoes. To be exact, Chuck Taylor canvas hi-tops that laced up to the ankle. He owned several different pairs, and today he had worn red. She removed the shoes with great care, replaced the mound of leaves at his feet, and parked her black penny loafers near his head. That way, she could find them later.

At twice the size of hers, Temple's shoes were mammoth. She untied the laces and slipped her foot inside one shoe. It dropped to the ground when she lifted her foot. Starting at the toe, she pulled the laces as tight as possible, working her way up to the ankle and then to the top. The big red shoes stayed on but were very floppy and clumsy. Her feet had become rubber rafts, ready for the rapids. As a circus member, she could have marched with the other clowns, she in her oversized clown shoes, furry pine needle legs and drenched rat look. But, all of that didn't matter now. Even wet, the Chuck Taylor canvas hi-tops that laced up to the ankle felt better than razor sharp pinecones, biting twigs and crunchy needles.

Time couldn't be wasted on aimless walking. She flopped up the riverbank, in search of a farm. She looked for a clearing in the woods. A clearing could mean people. A small clearing appeared around the next bend. After taking in a deep breath, she hugged herself for warmth and stomped clumsily along the riverbank toward the clearing, lifting one gigantic shoe after the other.

TWENTY-SIX

THE FARM

A wall of thick trees hid the farm from view. Old and dilapidated, the farmhouse had been built on a small plot of land cut from the dense woods. Long beams of split-rail fence lay broken along the overgrown dirt driveway. The small wooden house had once been coated with red paint, most of it now faded and peeling away from the wood, gathering in curls on the ground. A wrecked car, stripped of its parts, was parked on one side of the house. A maze of objects cluttered the yard. Everywhere the eye could see lay wheel rims, hubcaps, buckets, glass bottles, tin cans and other things now indescribable.

Erin suddenly felt anxious about voluntarily walking up to the property. The cracked sidewalk had broken into pieces, with large chunks out of place. Tall weeds brushed against her shoulders. A thistle with its prickly blossom scratched against her face. What had been the front lawn was now a natural prairie, with weeds and wildflowers blowing freely in the wind. Tall as she was for her age, she doubted anyone in the house could see her approaching.

The house appeared abandoned, except for smoke from the chimney. Jutting out from above the doorjamb were two rotten beams that had once supported a roof. The cement porch lay in ruins. Fully exposed to the weather, it supported a scrawny patch of weeds growing in the cracks. The broken picture window remained in place by virtue of masking tape. A rickety porch swing straddled the cracks in the cement. Only a dark, ragged hole remained in place of the doorbell. A crooked screen door hung loosely by one hinge still attached near the top of its rotting wood frame.

Erin pulled her mangled clothes into place and ran her fingers through her messy hair. After stepping carefully across the jagged chunks of cement, she lifted the red Converse shoes high in the air and stumbled up the stairs. From the looks of the place, she was certain her appearance wouldn't offend anyone, but she couldn't take the chance. Her grandfather repeatedly said, "Always put your best foot forward," but her feet were sore and tired and stuck in clown shoes. She wondered what grandfather would say now.

The frame of the screen door shook as she tapped on the wood and then waited for a response. A large yawn overcame her as she pounded a little harder on the front door. She tried to shake off the sleepiness, but it returned. Once again she set off the loud, clanking noise of the screen door rattling against the door jam with her knocking. She stepped back and waited. No one came.

An owl hooted in a nearby tree. The wind blew across the porch. She counted to twenty before knocking again. Still, no one answered. Erin thought she saw a corner of the front window curtain close. She knocked again, this time as loudly as she could. Pacing back and forth in her red clown shoes, she thought of kicking down the front door. She thought of jumping through the front window and grabbing the people inside. She thought of holding them by the collar and shaking them. Then she would turn them over and over, only stopping to stand them on top of their heads. Then she would scream at the top of her lungs until the house fell into tiny little pieces. She drew in a deep huff, ready to blow with the winds of a hurricane.

Then she saw herself inside her mind's eye. Superhero Olson stood ready with arms on hips, feet planted firmly in place, puffed cheeks ready for the challenge and wild eyes hunting for the prey. And with a flick of her pinky, her magical, super shoes would fly her through the air like speeding rockets and help her jump over tall buildings with a single bound and scale the tallest mountains.

Suddenly Superhero Olson was overcome by another yawn. Again, she stretched the sleepiness from her shoulders and smiled. Superhero Olson was just plain old tired and daydreaming again.

The dented brass knob wouldn't turn. She positioned her shoulder flat against the door, and pushed. It wouldn't budge. She stepped back, leaned in with all her weight, and rammed it. The door was surprisingly strong. It didn't move.

The remains of a sidewalk overgrown by weeds led around to the back of the house. A decayed staircase leaned against the back porch. Erin had to struggle to climb over the missing step, but she finally managed to get up to the back door and knock. An old rooster, perched on the back porch railing, met her eyes. He screeched, beating his wings furiously in the air. The bird wanted to fight. Turning her back on him, she knocked again.

"Hello . . . my name is Erin, and I have a friend who's been hurt . . . could you please open the door? I need to talk to you," she called out sweetly.

No one answered. The rooster became more frantic. His wings began beating faster. He lunged at her. Erin stared at the bird and then at the back door. The bird meant business. He lunged again, barely missing her with his beak. She flattened out against the opposite wall and tiptoed back down the steps, trying to stay clear of his attacks.

Once she was on the ground, the rooster relaxed and returned to his perched position. She surveyed the scene. Behind the house stood a lopsided barn, leaning to one side. The double doors were ajar. Perhaps an answer lay inside. She hurried toward the opening in the clumsy shoes.

A dim bulb hung over a copper contraption in the back of the room. The dark interior of the barn was vacant, except for the piled boxes along the wall. Neatly stacked bottles were stored underneath a wooden bench in the corner. Empty glass bottles littered the barn floor. Erin stepped over the containers and made her way toward the back.

The contraption was a copper kettle with copper tubing attached. The bright orange tubing coiled around like a pig's tail. A glass beaker caught the clear liquid dripping from the spout. An overpowering smell filled the air. It reminded Erin of the stuff used by her grandfather for cleaning wounds and sterilizing utensils.

She squinted at the kettle. Her eyes followed the coil tubing and the solitary drip hanging from the tip. Suddenly, she blinked and stepped back. This was an old-fashioned moonshine still! Grandfather said he knew of a man who had gone blind from drinking bad moonshine. Moonshine is the name used for homemade alcohol. And it was against the law to make your own alcohol! These were people who made and sold illegal moonshine! Erin looked around with a new awareness.

Grandfather said people could get hurt if they interfered with the moonshine business. This was a farm she wasn't supposed to find.

Her still-wet jeans made a whooshing sound as she scooted quickly toward the doors. If she hurried, she might be able to leave before they discovered she was there. Something caught her eye. Parked out of sight was what appeared to be a bright blue bathtub on wheels. It had been hidden by a stack of boxes.

Erin knew what it was immediately. It was an electric-blue ATV with a fiberglass body and four small over-inflated balloon-type tires. Only one person could sit in the front seat where the steering wheel was attached. A second seat of the same size was located directly behind. A total of two people could ride inside.

She grinned because this was something she knew about. Last summer, she had visited a farm where ATVs were used to bring in the cows. The dogs would start moving the cows back toward the barn from the fields, and the farm hands would ride out on ATVs to meet them. She drove one alongside her friends as they herded the cows to be milked across the fields and into the barn. The letters "ATV" stood for *all terrain vehicle*, a machine made to run in the mud, up hills, across the ground and, to a certain extent, even on water.

Erin gasped when she looked inside. Keys dangled from the ignition. A brown package sat in the back seat. Then she realized why these moonshiners would own an ATV. It could travel into places a car couldn't reach: through the woods, over creeks, up hills, and down trails. But what's more important, she realized, the ATV could take poor Temple home.

Trying to move quickly, without giving herself away, she lifted the clown shoes over the sides and took a place behind the wheel. The shoe's long, empty toe touched the gas pedal. When she pressed the shoe down, the pedal moved too. She chuckled to herself. Her legs were too short to reach the gas pedal, but the clown shoe wasn't.

The engine started with a turn of her wrist. The whirring sound grew louder as she pulled away from the wall and maneuvered around the boxes and empty bottles. Erin jumped out of the front seat and opened the barn door. Then she drove the ATV through the doorway and started down the overgrown sidewalk. The engine roared with every tap of the pedal, rocking back and forth as the tires climbed over the uprooted cement on their way past the back door.

Erin heard a noise from inside the house. The rooster started shrieking. Erin gripped the steering wheel with all her might. It was now or never. Now that they heard her, they would stop her any way they could.

She swung out away from the house, hoping to put as much space as possible between herself and whoever was now moving about inside the house. The engine roared as the ATV climbed the overgrown weeds and debris. The strong fiberglass body swayed like a carnival ride, waddling over lumpy ground and dips. The contents of the brown package made an awful racket in the back seat. As the ATV cleared the house, her eyes were fixed straight ahead, looking for the path into the woods, but an eerie feeling crept across her skin. A shiver suddenly ran up her spine, and she turned to look at the house.

The front door opened. Trying to gain more speed, Erin pressed harder on the gas pedal, steering straight through the wildflowers and five-foot weeds. The wheels of the ATV crushed the prickly thistle blossoms underneath.

Erin glanced back toward the house in time to see a strange creature jump from the front porch and start after her. Long gangly arms reached out from blue overalls. A hairy face turned toward her in rage. The thing roared, clumsily lumbering across the ground, throwing anything within reach. A hubcap flew through the air.

A tail pipe clipped Erin's shoulder. A bottle whizzed past her head. Shaken by the sudden turn of events, Erin stomped on the pedal and didn't look back. The edge of the clearing was straight ahead and the riverbank was next to that. All she had to do was keep her eyes on the road and hope an unexpected hole didn't send her flying into the air. The thickest part of the woods was within reach.

But the ATV didn't soar. It did not kick into warp speed and fly with the wind. It moved slowly up the steep bank, whining steadily in gear. Erin rocked forward trying to help it move faster. It had just cleared the steep hill and was leveling out on smooth ground, when a loud yell, like a warrior's call before charging into battle, came from behind.

The creature was advancing. The angry grunts grew louder as its long, giant strides brought it closer. A tin can bounced off her back. Erin tried pushing harder on the pedal, but nothing happened. Nothing happened at all. The ATV was now motionless. She checked her foot. The empty toe of the shoe no longer touched the pedal. It was bent out of shape and sticking straight up in the air.

There was only one thing left to do—slide down on her back, with her head underneath the steering wheel, and push the gas pedal with the heel of her foot. That meant not being able to see above the wheel. That also meant driving blind.

A bottle slammed into the back seat, shattering into bits of broken glass. A jolt rocked her away from the steering wheel. The creature, holding onto one side of the fiberglass body, tried to flip it over. Erin quickly slid below the wheel and jammed her heel up against the pedal. Before the creature could attack again, the ATV lunged forward with a sudden burst of energy and broke free. With her hand holding the bottom of the steering wheel, Erin guided the climbing ATV across the rough terrain and awkwardly weaved back and forth toward the river.

iNTO THE WOODS

The wall of thick bushes made a perfect hideout. Erin would be hard to find with all the trees and bushes surrounding her cozy little nest. The ATV had climbed up a steep and very muddy hill in search of a safe place. After clearing the farm and barely missing the river, she had found a thick branch that could push down on the gas pedal. But, the branch was bulky, and Erin could barely see around the bushy leaves blocking her face. Plus, the pedal had been difficult to control. The branch either punched the pedal flat against the floor or slipped and didn't give it enough juice. She had lurched continually back and forth until finding a hideout.

She parted the bushy wall of her hiding place and looked off toward the farm. The big, hairy creature had chased her as far as the river and then stopped when she darted into a thick grove of pine trees. Using her leafy branch like a broom, she had swept the pine-needle carpet back and forth until the tire tracks had disappeared from the ground. Completely hidden from view, Erin and the ATV waited inside a circle of bushes with the motor off.

She decided there was one thing she definitely had to do, before going any further: she had to switch shoes. The toe on the right clown shoe was pointing straight up in the air at a 90-degree angle. It no longer reached the gas pedal to push it down. And trying to use the branch to push the pedal wasn't working very well. That meant she had to switch shoes so the left shoe could do the work. Getting out of the woods would be impossible if she didn't.

The shoestrings had dried into stiff double knots and wouldn't give. She parted the bushes and checked once more for the creature. It wasn't safe to be in one place for too long. It would have been easy to push the pedal all the way down with the branch, and drive home, full speed ahead, but she couldn't leave Temple alone in the woods.

She dug at the strings. The knot became tighter each time she pulled up. Pinching the bottom strand with her fingernails, she expertly pulled it aside. A small strand gave way. The shoe came off after a yank requiring all her might. The left shoe proved to be more difficult.

Something snapped in the distance. She stopped to listen. A gray squirrel leapt across the treetops. She picked at the left shoelace repeatedly. Another suspicious sound erupted. Erin looked up wide-eyed. A second squirrel scampered across the treetops. Even with all the excitement, Erin felt herself yawning. The day had been long, she was weary, and her arms were made of Jell-O. Five-pound weights pushed against her eyelids, and her stomach growled in loud rumbling tones. Temple had devoured their snack while she watched for Billy Perez, and this morning she had left the house without breakfast. Lunch hadn't been any better. The pizza in the school cafeteria looked like pizza, but she knew from experience tasted like plastic, so she had pocketed her lunch money and gone to the library instead.

Except for the occasional squirrel, the woods remained calm. It had been some time now since Erin had left the farm. Either the creature had not followed or could not find her. Another yawn overtook her. She needed to rest her weary arms and bleary eyes for just a minute. Just a tiny second would be all she needed. A crow cawed . . . the wind blew gently across the ground . . . and she was blissfully relaxed . . .

The kitchen was filled with the lovely aroma of Sunday dinner. The dining room table was spread with steaming hot plates of mouthwatering food. A large platter of chicken, fried to perfection was accompanied by a boat of homemade gravy. Fettuccine noodles swam in a pool of creamy Alfredo sauce. A large dab of butter melted above the freshly picked green beans. A spiraling circle of steam floated above a hot loaf of bread. Two Dutch apple pies cooled on the windowsill. Her grandfather's freshly churned strawberry ice cream was chilling in the freezer. She drooled in anticipation of each scrumptious dish . . . noodles . . . ice cream . . . pie . . .

Suddenly, she was awake. She sat up and blinked. A disturbance in the woods had sent the squirrels running. The large bowl of Alfredo sauce with fettuccine noodles was gone . . . so was the sugar cone with the three scoops of Grandpa's strawberry ice cream. Her dream had vanished, and so had the feast. Her stomach growled in disappointment.

She parted the bushes. A gentle breeze continued to blow through the trees. The birds had stopped chirping. There was no movement in the woods at all, man or beast. She watched, waiting for a sign. There was only the restless swaying of the trees.

Her fingers attacked the laces with renewed energy. The sooner she got Temple home, the sooner she could eat. The left lace broke free, and she switched shoes without taking the time to brush the dirt from her socks.

Suddenly, a rustling noise echoed though the woods. The creature emerged over the hill. Erin froze in place. It was making its way toward her. Her heart started to pound. It stopped to study the ground, then moved slowly along the trail. She reached out for the ATV. The entrance faced the creature. If she were to go now, an escape would be possible, but the creature would see her. Then she thought of Temple. The creature might follow her through the woods like a cheetah at seventy miles an hour and discover her poor, injured friend. There was only one answer. Lie perfectly still and hope it walks by.

The creature crept forward, cautiously checking under every bush and looking behind every tree. Its long, bulky arms left a path of broken tree branches behind. Erin's heart pounded harder. The urge to run was overpowering. There was nothing to keep it from looking inside her little hideout. It would find her . . . and the stolen ATV—it's ATV.

Holding her breath, she checked on her secret weapon. Lying flat on her back, she quietly removed the wet, crumpled envelope containing the small plastic case from her pocket. She flipped the lid of the case open.

The creature let out a roar, and started toward her in great, leaping bounds. Erin didn't know what to do. Should she use her secret weapon or run? What if her secret weapon didn't work? What if the creature knocked it out of her hands? Suddenly the thought of staying vanished.

She closed the secret weapon's case, pushed it back in her pocket, jumped into the ATV, and turned the key. The engine coughed and sputtered but didn't start. Panic-stricken, she stomped on the pedal again, but this time the toe of the left shoe reached its mark, and the engine engaged with the sound of thunder. Slamming the shift into drive, she turned to see the creature appear from behind a bush. Its thick, heavy body lunged through the air. The ATV tore free of the clearing and the creature landed with a thud on the empty ground. Seeing the creature momentarily stopped, Erin raced for the thickest part of the woods.

TWENTY-EIGHT

THE SECRET WEAPON

The large, orange sun hovered low in the sky, the weakening rays filtering through the trees and across the ground. The temperature had dropped since the early afternoon. Already, a chill was beginning to creep through Erin's clothes. A strong, brisk breeze blew across the river. Leaves twirled in the air and waltzed along the horizon. She bounced up and down as if caught inside an amusement park ride. The ATV climbed easily over the uneven terrain and knotted tree roots, while she spun a web of different paths. Erin hoped the many trails would confuse the creature.

She hurried toward her injured friend. There were wild boars in the woods—wild boars with long pointed tusks sticking out from their snouts. These were fearsome beasts that gored their enemies to death. Her grandfather said thirty years had passed since a boar had been spotted, but that didn't make Erin feel any better. A frightening image of a wild boar rooting along the ground and stumbling upon her helpless friend haunted her mind. A quick push on the gas pedal threw the ATV forward.

Once around the bend, Erin made a straight line toward Temple. A branch crunched underneath as she pulled up alongside the mound of leaves. To her relief the manmade pile was undisturbed. It was exactly as she had left it. Jumping out, she quickly brushed the stray leaves from her friend's face. He was awake.

Temple struggled to open his glassy eyes. "Rinny, you wouldn't believe the dream I just had . . . I was caught inside a tornado and tossed around like a rag doll." One side of his mouth rose up in a faint smile. "Then something tickled my nose . . . couldn't scratch it."

Erin gently brushed a curl away from his forehead. "How do you feel? Do you remember falling in the river?"

His expression was blank at first. He raised an eyebrow. "Yeah, I was . . . trying to see you from the bank . . . you looked so stupid dipping your shoes into the river . . . you were covered in mud . . . then you were standing in the water . . . and you tried to put your wet socks on . . . and your shoes wouldn't fit . . . that was so funny . . . I started laughing . . . that's when I fell off the ledge."

"I heard you fall in," she said gently. "I jumped in to pull you out. Do you remember hanging onto my jacket?"

He moved his head groggily to one side. "It's kinda like a bad dream . . . I remember grabbing hold of something . . . I didn't want to let go . . . I was scared."

"Billy Perez helped pull you out," she said.

"He did?" he said slowly. "I heard a noise . . . saw Billy . . . I chased him."

"Never mind him, Temple," she said softly, stroking his arm. "I have some bad news."

He searched her eyes.

"You've hurt your leg, and that means we need to get you to a hospital."

He tried to sit up. "I don't feel hurt . . . in fact, I don't feel anything at all." The effort was too much. He lay down again. "Did you know your body goes into shock when it's been traumatized? You can't feel anything for a long time . . . I must be in shock."

"I can't explain right now, so please don't ask me any questions," Erin said hesitantly. Her eyes darted back and forth from Temple to the path she had just taken. "I can take you home in this ATV, but we need to leave now. *Right now, Temple.*" Her voice had picked up a tinge of panic. She tried to calm herself.

Temple stared at the ATV and then looked at her in confusion. "Go call my father. He'll come pick us up." He struggled to lean on his elbow. His eyes looked down at her feet. "Hey, aren't those my shoes? Why are you wearing them? And what did you do to that one? It looks like it's standing up at attention."

"Later," she whispered, "I'll have a lot to tell you after we get out of here. If I went somewhere now, it would be dark before I got back. I wouldn't be able to see. I really need your help. It's very important you get into the back seat of this ATV."

"Why?" he said stubbornly. "I don't really want to go anywhere. And I'm starting to feel really sick to my stomach . . . just call my father, and he'll come get me."

She stared at him in disbelief. There wasn't time for the whole story, and he wouldn't understand anyway. The creature had been fooled for a while, but Erin wasn't sure for how long. Temple would put on a brave face and try to protect her. He had always been the bravest person she had ever known, and the dearest, but she didn't want him to be brave now. She wanted him in the back seat of the ATV!

"Listen here, Temple," she said crossly. "I have to be back home before the sun goes down, or I'll be grounded. Is that what you want? There's no time to run after your father. This all terrain vehicle can carry us through the woods and out onto the paved road. It will take us home. I am starving, since you ate all of our food, and my grandfather is cooking hamburgers on the grill tonight. Now, get into the back seat before I get angry!"

Temple stared at her, half amused, half defeated. "Okay, Rin, for you. I don't want you to get into trouble."

He struggled to sit up. A mountain of leaves tumbled off to the side. A pained look masked his face as Erin lifted him slowly toward the ATV. He leaned wearily against the fiberglass body.

Erin tried wrestling the box from the back seat. The box had rattled all the way through the woods, and now she knew why. It was full of heavy bottles. She could barely lift it, and her arms weren't long enough to reach around the outside to get a good grip on it.

Temple struggled to keep his balance. The grimace on his face cut through her heart like a knife. He was in great agony, and she knew it. Summoning all her strength, she managed to roll the box over and push it up the side of the seat. It teetered on the outside rim before falling to the ground with a crash.

Temple's head bobbed up and down as if he were fighting sleep. He craned to see the box on the ground. Glass bottles tumbled from a split side, many of them broken into pieces. The clear liquid inside oozed out across the ground. The air smelled of alcohol, and Erin coughed. It was the homemade moonshine manufactured in the barn.

Erin whimpered silently to herself before checking for the creature. The coast was clear, but a new problem had appeared. The box had landed next to the tires. She pulled on the wet cardboard, trying to move it away from the wheels. It was still too heavy. She lightened the load by moving the unbroken bottles of alcohol and standing them upright on the ground. Gathering the shattered glass was the next thing to do. A flat tire would be disastrous, and they didn't have time for another disaster.

Suddenly, there was a thrashing noise in the woods. Erin looked up to see the creature charging toward them. It was advancing at an alarming pace, stomping on bushes and pulling off branches. Erin grabbed Temple by the arm and shoved. He screamed in pain as she hoisted his broken leg inside the back seat. Her heart sank with the agonizing sound, but she knew there was no time to be gentle. The creature was upon them.

She jumped behind the wheel and turned the key. The engine sputtered, and the smell of gasoline filled the air. She turned the key again. This time the engine started. She steered the wheel to the right, but a tree stood in the path. She started to go backwards, but the box was in the way, and thorny underbrush blocked their left side. She climbed out again. Temple moaned in agony. She kicked at the box, frantically trying to clear the way. A bottle inside exploded with a cracking sound. More alcohol oozed out through the sides.

Then the creature got her. Its long arms wrapped around her waist as it roared in fury tossing her violently back and forth. She gasped for breath with every squeeze of its powerful arms. A bottle broke abruptly across its back. It let go and Erin fell. Temple leaned over the side, swooped down for another bottle and lobbed it at the creature. Red with rage, the creature turned toward the ATV.

Erin fumbled inside her pocket, desperately hunting for the secret weapon. Her fingers locked on to it. She lifted the four-inch hatpin with the pearl top from the case. For years, her grandmother had lovingly pinned her hat to her hair with this pearl-tipped pin. The pin's four-inch steel shaft was thick and strong, and the tip as pointed as any needle. The large pearl on one end made it easy to hold.

The creature moved toward Temple but in defense, Temple launched another bottle at its head. The creature ducked and kicked the box out of the way. Temple hollered in pain as the creature caught hold of his arm. In blind hysteria, Erin sprang through the air and landed on the hulking back. She gripped the four inch steel shaft with her entire fist, jammed the hatpin into the creature's bottom and fell away to the ground. An ear splitting bellow tore from its lips. The creature circled around trying to reach its backside, like a cat chasing his tail.

Temple fell back in his seat. Erin jumped behind the steering wheel and rammed the gearshift lever into gear. The engine roared as she stomped on the gas pedal. "Hang on, Temple. Hang on, for dear life!" she screamed. Then the ATV shook roughly back and forth as it cleared the circling creature and drove out of sight.

TWENTY NINE
Big Mr. Smith

The morning sun filled the house with a brilliant light. Layers of white, billowing clouds stretched across the horizon. Birds chattered in the treetops. The individual honks from a flock of geese signaled the way to the pond. A gentle breeze blew through the air. It was a brand new day full of promise.

Erin combed her long brown hair into a high ponytail and then covered the orange hair tie with a pink scrunchy. She sipped from her glass of Grandfather's freshly squeezed orange juice, nibbled the edges of a poppy-seed bagel, and for a second time, read the letter she had just received. She leaned against her chair, and sighed. The telephone had not rung, and she was anxious. The nurse at the hospital had promised Temple would call before she left for school.

After mulling over every word, she placed the letter off to the side. Last night, the ride through the woods had been rough. Temple had been jerked back and forth in the ATV as they had climbed their way out of the woods. He had winced with every bump and groaned with every pothole, but he had never complained. She had parked the ATV at the hospital's emergency entrance, where the staff had lifted Temple onto a gurney. Dr. Gioia had examined Temple's leg and felt he would be able to run track again—but only after wearing a cast and doing special exercises. Temple had been relieved.

A deep yawn overcame Erin again, and she tried stretching the sleepiness from her bones. She returned to the morning newspaper. There was an interesting article about the President of the United States on the front page. The article told how the President calls on each senator personally and tries to persuade him or her into voting the President's way on important issues. If the President wants a certain tax, he might promise the senator an order to build more airplanes in the Senator's home state. It was very simple. The President would do a favor for the senator, and the senator would do a favor for the President.

She thought this over. There were things she could do for her classmates in return for votes, too. Charlotte Pillman was a good candidate for a complimentary homework pass, the one Erin had earned for being so prompt with her own assignments. And during the next week, she could take over Sean's job of feeding the turtles. She could wash the boards for Vicki, collect the homework for Eric, and straighten the bookshelves for Christopher. She could sweep the floor for Debra and pass out worksheets for Darchelle. And when she could afford it, she would give each kid in her student government a Blow Pop for working so hard.

But the whole thing was so puzzling. Weren't candidates voted into office for showing integrity and leadership skills—for making good decisions and working to make life better? She didn't know they were voted into office for the favors they passed out. And she always thought a student government should work together for everyone's sake, because that was their job—not because they were rewarded with Blow Pops. She chewed on her lower lip deep in thought. Maybe she didn't understand politics after all.

The phone rang. Temple's voice was cheerful on the other end.

"Temple, guess what!" she exclaimed, holding the letter in her hand. "Remember when Billy had an interview with the President? Well, awhile back, I wrote a letter to the President's opponent and asked him if he would visit our school. I wanted him to talk to the children . . . and he wrote back! He can't come because he is too busy, but he's sending his teenage daughter instead . . . and she's coming today and is going to speak in the auditorium with Billy and me!"

"That's great Rinny! I wish I could be there, but Dr. Gioia says I have to stay in the hospital," Temple said excitedly. "The Doc gave me one of those doctor frowns when I asked about leaving. But he did say that if everything turns out okay, I'll be home in time for your birthday party."

Picturing Temple's smile on the other end, Erin continued, "And he promised there wouldn't be any media, just like I asked, because he wants the students to know he cares about them and isn't using the opportunity to be on television. He says we children are the future, and he will always be there for us." Erin folded the letter and placed it in her pocket.

"That was a good idea to ask for no media. You don't want another disaster like before." Temple chuckled from his end.

"Don't worry, I'll tell you everything that happens. We didn't catch Billy in the act, but I think I have a good chance of winning anyway. Maybe you'll be calling me "Miss President" the next time we see each other." She broke out in a giggle.

Her backpack scraped against the door jam as she slid though the door in a rush. Today was not the day to be late. If she hurried, she might even break her old record to the school.

As she rounded the corner, Erin saw road construction blocking the two streets leading up to the school. The tops of both roads had been scraped away, leaving piles of gravel spread out along the surface. The paving crews were laying down fresh blacktop. A truck began to dump the sticky paving material in a pile. Erin looked in every direction. Orange ropes blocked the access from the sidewalks, but the quickest way to the school was through those two streets! She held her breath and ducked underneath the rope. A large bulldozer swung around and chased her back under. The man laughed at the horrified look on her face. Then he pointed to the detour sign. The walk had taken her four extra blocks out of the way. She didn't break her walking record, she didn't make it to school on time, and she almost missed being at the campaign table altogether.

Gasping for air, Erin finally stepped through the doors at Franklin Elementary. Outside the auditorium doors stood two tables. Mrs. Brambles directed her to the one on the right. Erin was to sit at one table and Billy at the other. After hurriedly scribbling her name on a piece of notebook paper, she folded it in half, and propped it up, like a pup tent. "Erin Olson, Presidential Candidate," it stated in different-colored inks. As candidates, she and Billy were to talk with each person as they approached the table.

Billy winked at her from his side of the room. Erin wanted to say thank you for helping at the river, but he turned away before she could

157

mouth the words. She frowned. Thanking him was going to be a difficult. Nothing was ever easy with him.

Just the thought of the coming event gave her goosebumps. The entire school had been invited to hear the last campaign speech. And that meant everyone would be able to meet her special guest. And since her class would be voting directly after the speech, it would be doubly hard for Billy to turn it to his advantage. This time, she had outsmarted Mr. Billy Perez. This time he wouldn't be able to spin or twist things his way. She chuckled to herself.

The candidates waited for the students from the various classrooms to arrive. The lobby started to fill. "What is a president?" asked a kindergartner. "Do presidents do homework?" asked a first grader. A second-grade boy told Erin she was pretty. A third-grade girl asked, "What does a president do?" Bernard-the-weasel stood at the far wall and gawked. Erin tried to ignore him. Students walked single-file into the auditorium. Friends waved as they passed the table. To her surprise, some of the boys gave her the thumbs-up. Charlotte Pillman hung in the background. When the rest of her class had finished, she stepped forward.

"Today's the big day," said Charlotte Pillman, her eyes twinkling.

Erin didn't know what to think. Charlotte was wearing a new dress, and her shiny hair was pulled back in a French braid. Charlotte was pretty, and Erin had never noticed—probably because she had never seen Charlotte smile before. She couldn't remember Charlotte ever being happy. That was how Charlotte Pillman had gotten her nickname in the first place. She was called "grouchy Charlotte Pillman" because she was *always* grouchy.

"Welcome back to school," replied Erin in her best politician voice. "You look very pretty today." She drew back instinctively waiting for the look. The last time she had paid Charlotte a compliment, she had been bombarded with fiery-hot laser beams and her "brain" eraser had been mysteriously shredded into crumbs.

Only Charlotte didn't give her the stare this time. Instead, she grinned and twirled around in her new dress. Erin blinked again, making sure this was the *real* Charlotte Pillman. This girl had stopped to talk *and* smile. But the *real* Charlotte Pillman was a bully—someone to avoid at all costs. It was the *real* Charlotte Pillman who had destroyed Erin's favorite box of pencils, the ones that looked like twenty-dollar bills and had cost her a week's allowance. Every time Erin stepped away from her desk, a pencil would be broken when she came back. She couldn't help but be suspicious.

"I have something for you, Erin," said Charlotte with a grin.

"Oh?" said Erin skeptically.

"I'm sorry I broke your favorite pencils. I did some extra chores to earn the money to replace them." Charlotte pulled out a small box of pencils and placed them on the table. There were twelve new pencils imprinted to look like hundred-dollar bills.

"Wow," whispered Erin. "Those are better than the twenty-dollar bills."

"I'm living in a new place now," Charlotte said. "My mother kicked me out of the house. I tried living down by the river but it got too cold, so I went to the police station. The courts said my mother wasn't well, and they placed me with a retired couple that wanted to help. I'm living with the Yorks now. Their children are grown, and they have a nice big house with lots of bedrooms."

Charlotte spun around a few more times, making her skirt billow up. Erin giggled at the sight. It was good to see Charlotte so happy.

"Mr. York drives me five miles to school, and Mrs. York packs my lunch and helps me get ready for school in the morning. When I get home tonight, we're doing homework together." Charlotte beamed. "I really love it there."

Reaching out to shake Charlotte's hand, Erin told her how happy she was that Charlotte was doing so well. Erin had always lived with a loving family and a grandfather who watched out for her. She was fortunate. And there was Teddy her cat, the most adorable pet in the world. She knew Charlotte Pillman would be all right now. "Do you have a pet?" she asked hopefully.

Charlotte chuckled. "A brand new puppy named Kat. I got to name her. I want you to know, I'm voting for you today. You are one of the kindest girls I know."

Erin started to say thank you, but Charlotte twirled away and disappeared into the auditorium. She turned the pencils over in her hands. Maybe Charlotte wasn't so bad after all, she thought. Charlotte wasn't grouchy Charlotte Pillman anymore, and she wasn't poor Charlotte Pillman either. Now she was just Charlotte Pillman—Erin's friend.

The auditorium began to fill with children. Billy sat at his table mobbed by a group of boys. Erin had hoped to speak with him. She wouldn't be able to rest until she did so. Billy had turned out to be a good candidate, and more important, he had stepped forward when it really counted.

"Erin, I would like to see you," said an unexpected voice.

Erin turned to see her grandfather standing at the table. He turned his cap over and over in his hands. He only did that when something was on his mind. She squinted at him. Something must have been terribly wrong. Her grandfather never interrupted a school day. He believed educating your mind was one of the most important things a person could do.

"There is someone I would like you to meet . . . and I also believe you owe him an apology," he said. His voice was firm and loving—but disapproving.

The creature from the farm stepped around the corner and into the room. Only he wasn't a creature, but a giant man with dark, weathered skin and deep wrinkles. A long, bushy beard covered his face, and the gray hair flowing from the top of his head reached down to his waist. His small, narrow eyes looked sadly at her.

Her first reaction was to run. The panic she had felt in the woods bubbled up inside her. She had to hide; she had to find a safe place. If she ran into the auditorium, the creature wouldn't be able to find her. If she ran through the school doors, she could hide in her favorite place on the playground. The place no one knew about. If she just stood there, the creature would grab her for sure. Her eyes darted from the man to her Grandfather. Then she saw the calmness in her grandfather's eyes. She realized she wasn't in the woods anymore. She was at Franklin Elementary with her grandfather and hundreds of kids.

The man opened his hand and held out the pearl-tipped hatpin.

"This is Elijah Smith, Erin, and he wanted to return your grandmother's hatpin, to you," stated her grandfather. "When I returned the ATV to the farm this morning, I met Mr. Smith. He's deaf, honey. He can't speak very well, but he can read lips if you talk slowly. You frightened him last night, and that's why he didn't answer the door. He lives in the woods because he doesn't get along well with strangers. I'm afraid he doesn't really understand outsiders."

Erin's shoulders sagged, and her heart suddenly felt heavy. She stared glumly at the tabletop. Last night, he had been a creature with a hairy body and a monstrous roar, and she had smote the monster with her secret weapon and saved Temple from doom. She had arrived home a hero. But now her monster was deaf . . . and afraid of her! Things had suddenly gotten a lot worse.

Her grandfather rubbed her back. "Elijah thought you had stolen his all terrain vehicle. He was chasing you because he thought you were a thief. He didn't understand what had happened until I arrived this morning and explained it to him."

"But I saw a moonshine still in his barn, and there was a box full of moonshine in his ATV," she whispered, carefully avoiding Mr. Smith's eyes.

Her grandfather took hold of her hand. "Mr. Smith makes his own alcohol. He's from the Deep South, and his family has always made what they call *medicine*. He makes it only for himself."

Erin didn't feel any better. Her throat had a knot in it.

"He says he knows why you stuck him with the hatpin. He understands that you were afraid of him. He has told me how sorry he is that things turned out this way. Now, do you have something to say to Mr. Smith?"

She swallowed and, looking down at the floor, offered her hand to the man she had thought was a creature. She looked into Elijah Smith's unhappy eyes. "I am very sorry for upsetting you yesterday. I didn't mean to scare you, but your ATV helped my best friend get to the hospital, and we both thank you. I'm especially sorry about the hatpin."

Elijah Smith's eyes sparkled with approval. His warm expression and gentle handshake confirmed that he was not the creature she had thought him to be. She pinned her secret weapon to her dress and squeezed his hand in thanks. His cheeks turned red under the bushy beard.

Her grandfather kissed her on the cheek. "I'm going to take Mr. Smith home now. Tomorrow is your birthday and we'll do something extra special. I've spoken with Temple and he says not to start without him. I'm very proud of you, young lady. Now go into the auditorium and get yourself elected." He gave her a hug before escorting Mr. Smith out the front door.

Billy approached her table. "Going in, *Rinny?*"

"Only Temple is allowed to call me 'Rinny,'" she replied, tartly. Any kind thoughts of talking to him had vanished.

"I know," he said, teasingly. "But I like the sound of '*Rinny*'. Seems to suit you." He grinned, gave her a wink and strolled into the auditorium.

THIRTY

THE Special Guest

The large room clamored with excitement. Each class moved single-file into the long rows of seats, while the teachers sat on the aisles. Mr. Cohen strolled through the room, checking on the activity. Two local policemen stood at the doorways, watching the crowd. A large group of adults filled the balcony and lined the auditorium walls. A podium with a mounted microphone stood center stage, the bright balcony lights encircling the stand. Erin and Billy took their seats onstage next to the platform on which the podium stood. A third chair was left empty.

Erin felt suddenly nervous. The first speech in the classroom had been a disaster, but she knew what to do now. Don't try to be funny, because humor isn't the same for different groups of people—a comedian on television had said that. When a joke fails, it leaves the speaker feeling very foolish. Be very clear about what you say, and watch the audience to see if they understand your message. Stand up straight, be respectful, and ignore the troublemakers—like Billy's friend, David. The last time she had spoken, he had kept a finger up his nose. Afterwards, ask the audience if they have any questions—that way you know about any confusion or misunderstandings.

Erin looked again at the kids in the front row. Bernard-the-weasel was staring at her with an open mouth and clutching her pink pencil against his heart. Lately, he had been everywhere. It seemed to her as though each time she looked out the window at home, he was strolling by. When she ate lunch at school, he was watching. When she walked down the hall, he was behind her. She thought she had been imagining things before, but now she was sure she had seen his face among the crowd at the tin mine, too. And trying to ignore the pitiful sight staring at her now wasn't working. For some unexplainable reason, every time she looked away, she was drawn back to his gawking face. And then he would smile, thinking she was interested in him.

A teenage girl approached the stage. Her short black hair hung in ringlets around her face. She wore a bright yellow dress and her large blue eyes crinkled when she smiled. But it was the black penny loafers that made Erin smile. The copper heads twinkled when she walked.

"Hello, I'm Christina," said the girl to Erin and Billy. "Thank you for inviting me to your school. My father was very excited when he received your letter, Erin. It reminded him of when he was a schoolboy."

Billy glanced sideways at Erin. He was confused. She chuckled softly to herself, before accidentally facing Bernard-the-weasel again. He was drooling.

"You're the Presidential candidate's daughter?" asked Billy in a bewildered voice. "*The* Christina Schmidt? The one with the famous guinea pig who loves pizza?"

Erin snickered to herself. "I invited Christina to speak today. She's going to tell us about her father and life as a real campaigner. Her father wrote that she is on the campaign trail with him and has a special tutor to teach her school lessons. Normally he doesn't like his daughter to campaign alone, but he said Christina has a mind of her own, and she insisted on coming."

Christina shook hands with both of the candidates before taking the vacant seat. Billy looked dreamily at the special guest. Bernard-the-weasel stared shamelessly at Erin. She had hoped Temple might have talked himself out of the hospital, but he was nowhere to be seen. She needed him to sit next to Bernard.

Mr. Cohen approached the podium, tested the microphone by reciting the numbers "one, two, three," and then hushed the audience. He removed a note from his new sports jacket and began to speak. "I want to introduce our two fifth-grade candidates from Mrs. Brambles' class: Billy Perez and Erin Olson."

The children clapped politely. The candidates waved.

Mr. Cohen continued, "There will be a vote taking place in Mrs. Brambles' classroom directly after our assembly today. Voting is part of a democratic election. That means each person in that class will choose one of these two students to be president. Each person will vote by casting a ballot. Each will check off, in private, which candidate he or she wants and then drop the secret ballot into a box. When all the votes are counted, the person with the most votes wins."

Billy lifted his arms up, acting as though he was the winner. The children giggled. Mr. Cohen turned around, but Billy pretended to be listening intently.

Mr. Cohen continued, "But before that happens, both Billy and Erin will be giving their final speeches to us, today. Each will try to convince us why he or she should be president."

Billy stepped to the front of the stage and bowed. The children broke into a giggle again. Mr. Cohen turned to give Billy a disapproving look. Billy grinned at the audience before returning to his seat. Erin watched him with apprehension.

"But first, I have a treat for you," said Mr. Cohen with pride. "Erin Olson has invited a very special guest to be with us today. The lovely young lady sitting next to our candidates is Christina Schmidt, Dr. Stephan Schmidt's daughter. As you know, Dr. Schmidt is campaigning to be the next President of the United States. You may have seen Christina on the news, standing next to her father at the rallies. You might remember that she is not alone on the campaign trail. Her pet guinea pig, Arnold, is also traveling with her."

Applause filled the auditorium. This was a famous celebrity. This was the young trailblazer, the girl in the news every day. This was also the girl who had asked the president of Russia to play a game of chess. In fact, this was the girl who had beaten the president of Russia at a game of chess. This was also the girl who had agreed to a rematch after the election. Mr. Cohen escorted Christina to the microphone.

Christina asked the children to stand. "I want you to reach up to the sky, then bend down and touch your toes as fast as you can, ten times, and then sit down."

The children gladly did as they were told.

"Good," she cooed. "Now, you won't be a bunch of wiggle worms while I'm talking."

The auditorium bubbled with chuckles. She began with a loud hello, and then addressed each class by grade. She thanked Erin for the invitation, Mr. Cohen and the teachers for their dedication to education, and the guests standing in the back of the room and sitting in the balcony for coming. Then she began to tell her story.

As a student, she studies the same subjects as other children. Spelling and math are her favorites. She loves to read books and finds herself in constant trouble for talking too much. She plays the violin and clarinet, and she swims whenever possible.

"That's when I'm not campaigning with my father," she said proudly. "Right now, I'm traveling around the country and speaking to people about my dad. It's very hard work, being on the campaign trail. We never take a day off and work from the minute we get up until the minute it's time for bed.

"Can you imagine? The alarm rings, you get up and get dressed, and someone is waiting for you. You speak to a crowd, pose for a few photographs, speak to the reporters, and then rush off to another place and do the same thing all over. Then it's time for schoolwork. You go to bed, and you wake up the next day and start all over.

"We keep up this pace because my father wants to talk to all the people, but there isn't time, so I help him by going to places to speak for him. This is a big country, you know. He wants our schools to be the best they can be, and he wants every one of you to have the opportunity to learn. He was especially excited about Mrs. Brambles' fifth-grade class having an election, because that's where democracy begins. Having the right to select a leader is the American way. People sharing and working together make a strong society, and a strong society means a strong nation."

The students were listening quietly to everything Christina said. Some of the adults had moved closer to the stage. The teachers smiled contentedly, and Mr. Cohen beamed in the front row.

"Some people only do things for money or because other people are watching," Christina said. "But a good leader does things simply because they need to be done . . . not because somebody has a camera and promises to put the person's picture in the paper. A good leader does something *because it is the right thing to do.*" This type of leader is rarely seen. These are the people who quietly get things done and go about their own business, never drawing attention to themselves. My father refers to them as the country's unsung heroes."

Mrs. Brambles nodded in agreement.

Christina turned toward Erin. "This is not the first time my father has run for President," she said, turning back toward the audience. "He ran for president of his fifth-grade class too . . . "

Erin looked surprised. She didn't know Dr. Schmidt had run for president when he was in school.

"I'm afraid he lost, but it taught him an important lesson," Christina said with conviction. "He didn't lose because he didn't have what it takes; he just didn't win that particular race. There is a great difference between being a loser and losing a race. I want everyone to think about that."

Erin watched the children, looking for any kind of signs. Her class clapped every time Christina paused to take a breath. The adults in the back of the room applauded at the end of nearly every sentence. "Yes," she whispered . . . Christina was a hit. Erin had moved to the head of the race. Giddy with glee, she absent-mindedly glanced at Bernard-the-weasel. He blew her a kiss. She scolded herself and pledged not to look again.

Christina looked directly at Erin again. "He kept working on the things he believed in and became the senior class president in high school, then the class president in college and later, the founder and president of his own company. Later, he became the governor of his state. He says it's not the winning and losing . . . it's what you do that counts. So remember, not every hero shines, and being a leader is not about winning a race. Thank you very much for sharing your time with me today."

She waved to the children as she stepped down from the podium and onto the stage with Erin and Billy. A woman in a blue business suit handed her a bundle. Christina turned and lifted Arnold, her guinea pig, high into the air. The children shrieked with delight. Arnold's orange-and-black legs kicked in the air. The people rose to their feet. The applause was overwhelming.

Erin clapped enthusiastically. Billy whistled.

Christina stopped to squeeze Erin's hand. "My father sends these words," she whispered. "*Never, never give up.*"

Christina turned toward Billy. He kissed the back of her hand and lifted it high in the air like awarding first place to a champion. His smile stretched from ear to ear. The children roared with laughter. Mr. Cohen rushed to the front of the stage. Billy acted like his heart was breaking when Christina descended the steps. His empty arms reached out for her as she walked away. Erin couldn't help but frown.

Billy stood at the edge of the stage, motioning for all the students to sit down. The auditorium became quiet again. He took the microphone off of the podium and walked freely across the stage. "I don't know about you, but I think I'm in *love* . . . "

Laughter broke out again. The fifth-grade boys let out whooping calls. The teachers wagged their fingers. Mr. Cohen turned around, and the room became instantly still.

Billy passed an opened hand across his face, and his mischievous grin turned to a no–nonsense expression. He bowed before beginning to speak.

"I have a few ideas I want you to hear. " He signaled for the lights to go out. The slide show came on, and a newly designed playground with enclosed tunnels showed across the screen. The red, yellow and blue tunnels looped around into a maze of crawling fun. "I have a plan that involves the entire school in fund-raising. With everyone's help— we can put this new playground on school property by spring."

The children squealed with delight. Erin stared at him with wide eyes. Billy Perez had outdone himself. The Tootsie Pops were one thing, but a new playground? Her mind raced trying to decide what to do. There was still time to think of something spectacular.

Next, he talked about the wasted talent at school and how he as the leader could take the class in a new direction. The vacant lot next to the school was available, and Mr. Cohen had agreed to let the fifth-grade class grow vegetables. The class would sell the produce as a lesson in economics. The money was to go toward a historical tour of Washington, D.C., where the President was expecting them for a private tour of the White House. And the White House kitchen was going to prepare the President's personal recipe for chocolate chip cookies— the all you-can-eat variety.

The students cheered. All three fifth-grade classes jumped to their feet in applause. Bernard's class hooted and hollered until they realized Billy wasn't talking to them. They reluctantly sat down, realizing they had been left out of the fun. Billy bowed several times before returning to his seat. Erin pretended to approve, her lips stretched into a plastic grin.

The noise finally died down with the help of the teachers. Erin shook Billy's hand before clearing her throat and stepping up to the podium.

"I want to thank Mrs. Brambles for having this election. I will write to candidate Schmidt, thanking him for sending his daughter to us and letting us be part of the campaign. But first, there is something I need to say. When Mrs. Brambles first announced Billy Perez as a candidate for president of the class, I was shocked. To me, Billy couldn't possibly be a good leader . . . everyone knows Billy is the king of the class clowns."

Erin expected Billy to get upset when she mentioned the class clown thing, but he was grinning with pride. She hesitated before starting again.

"But I was wrong. Billy has changed. Yesterday, my friend Temple Black was in trouble. Temple fell into the rapids . . . " She paused to draw in their attention. "That's why he isn't here today."

A hush fell across the crowd. Bernard-the-weasel moved to the edge of his seat. Charlotte Pillman's eyebrows went up. The adults were focused on her. Mrs. Brambles leaned forward. Every eye in the room was facing the podium.

"As you know, the current in the river is strong. It kept pulling Temple under so he couldn't breathe . . . and I was really scared, because the river was stronger than anything I've ever seen. Then something happened . . . Billy Perez showed up."

All heads turned toward her opponent. Billy gazed sheepishly at the floor, his face beginning to turn red. Erin could see the corner of his mouth turned up in a grin.

"I caught Temple as the rapids pushed him by the river bank, but the current was too powerful. It kept tugging at him, and I couldn't hold on anymore. My arms were dying . . . and just when he started to slip away, something happened. Billy Perez reached into the water and helped me drag Temple up to safety. I want to thank Billy Perez today for his help . . . If Temple were here, he would say the same thing."

Erin turned toward Billy and began to clap. The children joined her. Billy looked out with an awkward smile. Mr. Cohen and Mrs. Brambles nodded at each other with approval. The school reporter wrote everything down in his book. Bernard looked amorously at her, but Erin didn't care. Christina had spoken, the school had loved her and she had done the right thing by thanking Billy. Happy with the turn of events, she placed her speech on the podium. It was time to begin.

"I would like to talk today about what a tremendous responsibility it is . . . "

Suddenly, the microphone went dead and her voice fell flat in the air. Before she could blink, the lights went out, and the auditorium broke into chaos. Squeals broke out in the dark. The principal's voice rose above the confusion as he ordered two students to open all the curtains. The many windows of Franklin Elementary lit the school with natural sunlight. Mrs. Brambles held up two fingers, and the other teachers followed. The room became silent. Because of unforeseen technical difficulties, the students were dismissed and sent back to their classrooms. Billy and his friends chortled all the way up the steps.

THIRTY-ONE

A Row of Tootsie Pops

Charlotte Pillman, leaning on her newly scrubbed desktop, smiled at Erin when she took her seat. The new Charlotte held two crossed fingers in the air. The assembly was over, and Mrs. Brambles had scheduled the presidential vote to take place during Social Studies class. Erin viewed all the Tootsie Pops in the room. Each student had one. Row after row of the little white sticks bobbed up and down from long rows of lips. Erin twirled her own purple grape pop between her fingers.

Billy had made it to the classroom door before anyone could enter the room. With a jumbo bag of Tootsie Pops tucked under his arm, he had given out two to each passing student. Charlotte Pillman had a chocolate mustache. Even Mrs. Brambles was nursing a red cherry pop.

Erin sighed and took out her Coca-Cola pen. The campaign was almost over. Campaigning had been exhausting and expensive. All her money had been used for posters and supplies, and last night she couldn't sleep because she was worried about the vote. A large yawn punctuated her struggle to stay awake.

"Erin and Billy, I want to commend you for a job well done. And Erin, thanking Billy for saving Temple's life was a very mature thing to do, and especially touching." Mrs. Brambles spoke from behind her desk.

"But, Mrs. Brambles, that wasn't my speech . . ." Erin said, frantically raising her hand.

"Now class, it is time for our vote," interrupted the teacher. Benjamin Franklin reading spectacles sat perched on the end of her nose.

Erin squirmed in her seat, trying to catch the teacher's attention.

"And children," said the teacher, "we must work quickly, because our time is very limited. We are far behind in our schedule, and I have scheduled a guest speaker to come in and tell you about being an author."

Erin slumped over in her chair and stared at the motionless Coca-

Cola pen. Her moment to speak had vanished.

"This is the format agreed upon by the campaign committee," Mrs. Brambles said. "We will start with the front row. One person at a time will approach my desk, check off the person he or she wants for president, then place his or her folded paper into the shoebox. After that, take your seat again. Read silently to yourself until everyone has voted and I have counted all the ballots."

Erin flicked her pen open and shut, over and over again. Her row was first. Charlotte Pillman would vote first, and she was counting on Charlotte's vote. She pulled her favorite book, out of her desk and set it on her desktop. *Witches*, by Roald Dahl, had been purchased with her own money. The first row finished voting and the students returned to their seats. A Sherlock Holmes bookmark guarded Erin's place in her book. The bald witches with square feet were spitting blue ink. For a short time, she was lost inside Roald Dahl's magical world of wonder. The witch had just turned a little boy into a mouse, when Mrs. Brambles spoke again.

"I have been very pleased with our lesson on democracy. We have learned some valuable lessons as a class."

Erin searched the teacher's face. Mrs. Brambles glanced around the room, but didn't look at her or Billy. Then she re-counted the votes and, after pushing her chair back from the desk, stood at the front of the class. Erin sighed. Mrs. Brambles was cool as a cucumber.

"The voting was very close," she said. "The winner only won by one vote. There was a write-in vote for Teddy the cat."

The students roared. "Who voted for Teddy the cat?" Erin demanded to know as she turned toward the back row. The boys doubled over with laughter. She frowned at Billy, who was beet red with the giggles. Squeezing her pen, she turned toward the front again.

"Mr. Cohen wanted both candidates to know he is pleased with all the effort and feels our class has been a good example to the school." The teacher picked up the ballots from her desk.

Charlotte held her thumb up. The girls smiled when Erin glanced across the room. Even the boy reporter grinned at her. One boy stuck out his tongue; another boy pulled down the bottom of his eyes and pushed his nose up. A third boy hung pencils from his ears until Mrs. Brambles cleared her throat; then the pencils fell out. Billy winked, and Mrs. Brambles looked at each of them with a smile.

"I counted the votes twice, because the tally was so close," the teacher said reassuringly.

Erin scribbled furiously on the front of her notebook.

"Class," Mrs. Brambles said, "your new president is Billy Perez."

Erin gulped and stared at the blackboard. Her Coca-Cola pen rolled off the side of the desk and fell with a clunk against the wooden floor. A knot formed in her throat. She fought back the tears. The class couldn't see her cry, no matter what. Presidents don't cry, at least not in public. But then she suddenly looked down. It didn't really matter because she wasn't a president.

She placed her head down on the desk. A commotion broke out in the back of the room. Her vision became blurry as the tears started to well up. Billy-the-Silly Perez had been formally elected president of the class. Now he was a king and a president: king of the clowns and president of the class. A tear splashed on her desktop. She quickly wiped her eyes against a sleeve.

Charlotte patted her on the back and whispered how sorry she was. The boys in the back of the room yelled "hooray" in unison. Some of the students gasped. Erin looked up. Each boy in the back of the room took turns trying to wrestle the new president to the ground, but Billy triumphed. Mrs. Brambles tapped against her desk with a ruler.

Erin leaned all the way back in her chair, teetering dangerously back and forth on the two back legs. So, what if teetering back and forth was a good way to fall? She didn't care. Let fate tip her over. She would just get up again.

Then she remembered the determination on Billy's face when Temple was in the water, and how he had changed since the beginning of the campaign. He had become a good student and had stopped most of his clowning around. He was actually likable now. And she had noticed the way Mrs. Brambles was pleased with him, not to mention Mr. Cohen's relief.

"Billy, have you decided on a vice president?" asked the teacher.

"Yes, I have," he replied.

The boys looked expectantly at their king. Three girls batted their eyes. Billy strolled past Erin's desk and stood before the class. He didn't look at her as he pondered what to say next. He rubbed his chin several times in deep thought.

"I've thought a lot about this," he said solemnly. "Some of you think of me as a clown, but I really wanted this job, and you'll see that I am a good leader. Then I asked myself, who would I want for president, if not me. I didn't want you, David, because you snore during silent reading."

David turned red. The class laughed.

"Sorry, David," he said with a chuckle, "I was just kidding. I thought of everyone I know and kept coming back to the same person. There was never any question about it. I want Erin Olson to be my vice president."

A chair crashed to the floor. No one missed Erin Olson falling over backwards in surprise.

THIRTY-TWO

The Last Clue

The birds chirped outside the bedroom window. Teddy rolled over on his back and purred affectionately. Erin folded her hands behind her head and stared up at the ceiling from her bed. The new 'Nsync disc had just finished playing. Today was her birthday, and the CD was a present from her father.

She was wearing a white dress, also new, that looked like a long tennis shirt. It had been hanging in her closet this morning when she awoke. Below the dress were sparkly shoes with two-inch block heels. They were shoes just like Dorothy's in the *Wizard of Oz*.

The public library had been full of books on Codes, Ciphers, Cryptograms, Palindromes, and Anagrams. Now a large stack sat on the stand next to her bed. Last night she had combed every page until she had broken the code.

She could laugh about the adventure now. Every clue had been faithfully followed, beginning with the trip to the cemetery. Once inside the graveyard, she had been attacked, tied up and bagged, just as planned. The second clue, found inside a mysterious package left on her doorstep with no return address, gave her a riddle to solve. That riddle had taken her inside a closed mine, a dark and damp cavern where she had pulled a rotting cat's head out of the rocks. Her hand curled up instinctively just thinking about it.

Then Temple had discovered a locket that belonged to her down in the mine. Inside was a picture of Miss Haggerty, the old maid living in the haunted mansion. Erin and Temple had set out during a thunderstorm to ask the old woman about her connection to the locket. The old woman had answered with her cane. Winston, the butler, had seen a boy following them in the rain. She had known the boy had been Billy.

But when they were preparing to leave the mansion, Winston had handed over a pink envelope directing them to the last clue, which had been written in code. Braving the rapids to rescue Temple and stumbling through the woods in oversized clown shoes hadn't been part of the game. Neither had driving a stolen ATV across the woods like a racecar driver and battling a giant deaf man. She cringed at the thought of poor Mr. Smith. He had been an unexpected victim.

The campaign and mysterious trail of clues had kept her so busy, she had lost track of her birthday. Today the family would arrive for the famous birthday meal prepared by her grandfather every year. As always, Grandfather had let the birthday girl decide on the menu. And as always, she had chosen ribs stewed in home-made spaghetti sauce and served over angel hair pasta, and of course, carrot cake with cream cheese icing. Not just any cream cheese icing, either. It had to be the real kind, made from scratch. The house would fill with aunts and uncles and cousins.

A vase full of pink carnations sat on her dresser top, compliments of Bernard-the-weasel. Erin had no idea how he had known it was her birthday, for she certainly hadn't told him. Her father had polished the rose-gold locket, replaced the chain with a new one, and inserted a picture of Teddy on one side and Erin's family on the other. A book, *The History of America*, was signed, "With love, from Grandpa."A plate-sized chocolate chip cookie from the mall said, "Happy B' Day, From Prez Perez."

The downstairs doorbell rang.

"Erin, Temple's here," called out her grandfather.

Teddy meowed softly as Erin checked herself quickly in the mirror. Today her long brown hair draped softly across her shoulders. She fastened the locket around her neck and squirted a touch of her mother's expensive perfume on her wrist. After all, it was her birthday. Then she raced down the steps, two at a time. Temple stood at the bottom on crutches. His black, curly hair flopped back and forth as he struggled to hold his balance.

"Hi, Rinny," he said with a smile. "I'm sorry you lost the election. You deserved to be president."

She looked down. "Billy chose me to be vice president." Then she looked up with a wide grin. "He doesn't know it yet, but I have a list of

176

things that are going to be done. I just have to figure out how."

They laughed together.

The doorbell continued to ring as relative after relative arrived. Erin led Temple into the sunroom. The autumn sun fell across the pine paneling, creating a cozy atmosphere. Grandfather had set snacks in the living room for all to enjoy, but everyone gravitated toward the kitchen. The kitchen became noisy with chatter.

Erin and Temple were left to themselves. Temple propped his crutches against the end table and leaned back in the wicker chair. Grandfather appeared with a tray of punch, and then scampered off to the kitchen to guard the sauce. Uncle Lonnie was famous for helping himself to all the goodies when no one was around.

"How do you feel?" Erin asked.

"Better than the other night," he said with a snort, before rubbing the back of his head. "I have a slight headache from our wild ride through the woods . . . you were a maniac, hitting every tree root in the place."

"It was getting dark, and I was in a hurry," she said teasingly. The pink egg was cradled in her hands. "You know," she began, "I've always complained about Billy Perez being the king of the clowns. And when Mrs. Brambles announced him as my opposition, I naturally thought the worst. Just think about it . . . that afternoon, a dead rat is dropped on my doorstep. It's just the kind of thing Billy would do, tying a note to such a creature. Next, I'm attacked in the cemetery . . . I accused him in front of the class, but, naturally he denied it."

"Well, what did you expect him to say, Rinny?" mused Temple. "Yes, he had sacked you so you would drop out of the race? Remember, the principal, all the students and Mrs. Brambles were watching him."

"I know. I was stupid and didn't think it through . . . I learned my lesson," she repeated, positively. "You see, the note attached to the rat was really confusing. And I hadn't heard the doorbell . . . but that's because it wasn't a doorbell, at all. It was a knock."

Temple's eyebrows rose.

She grinned, rolled the pink egg over in one hand, and slowly sipped the punch she held with the other. "When we arrived at the cemetery, you went one way and I went another. I was all alone when someone tied me up and bagged me, but I wasn't hurt because that was never the intention."

"I believe you're right," Temple said amiably. "That was my assessment too, My Lady."

"I tried to call for help but couldn't. Suddenly, the person disappeared, and you showed up out of breath. The funny face drawn on the outside of the bag was just the sort of thing Billy would do. In the classroom, he was doodling on my poster at every chance. On the way home, I agreed when you said we shouldn't tell anyone. We didn't want to complicate things."

"That was the logical thing to do. We didn't know what was going on, yet," he said thoughtfully, sipping his punch.

"And then we discovered the Chinese boxes," she said. "We both examined the box, trying to unravel the mystery. I rubbed the wax with paper and pencil and discovered the letter "B." I can see now, I was never meant to discover that, because it definitely was a clue, although I didn't realize what kind of clue at the time. You insisted I was wasting my time.

"Then I caught Billy in his ski mask looking through the kitchen window, and I was convinced he really was following me."

Temple nodded with each comment.

"Then there was the mine . . . you and I entered it together, with only our flashlights against the pitch dark. My hand was stuck inside a hole while you looked elsewhere. Always good at hide-'n'-go-seek . . . you found the locket. And the locket? I figured out how Billy had climbed into my room and searched through my belongings."

"Which was very possible, Rin. You do leave your bedroom windows unlocked," added Temple earnestly.

"Yes, that's true," she stated slowly. "But, the tree is too far from the window sill for anyone to use as a ladder."

"Correction, Rin. It's too far for you," added Temple.

"But then, there's the pink letter we picked up at the haunted mansion . . . where Miss Haggerty didn't know anything about our problem. I love the color pink and everyone knows it," she reflected, "so using pink paper wasn't much help."

"True. Pink and the name Rinny Olson go together, hand in hand," he added with a chuckle.

"By this time, I realized something else might be going on. I didn't really believe it, though, because I couldn't drop my guard. I needed to catch Billy in the act."

"Oh?" said Temple. "What do you mean?"

"You'll see," she said holding her head high. "The final clue was hidden on General Taylor's statue. You thought it was too dangerous for me to climb. Well, I climbed it anyway, but I couldn't find a clue . . . of course, I could only check the bottom part of the statue. Then you climbed up and found something inside the bird's nest . . . that something turned out to be this pink plastic egg. It was pink because I like pink, and it was plastic to protect it from the weather. Of course, maybe the person wasn't really worried about the weather at all. Maybe the clue had just been placed there."

Temple whistled. "Really? Boy, you have been thinking about this." He folded his arms.

"And then I saw Billy from the statue. I saw him the first time in the kitchen window, and Winston spotted him the second time at the Haggerty mansion. And I know, I heard him at the mine . . . so, I wasn't surprised when he showed up at the statue. I thought we had him then. I thought for sure I would win the race."

"Billy did seem to be everywhere," agreed Temple.

"But of course, you didn't catch him. I wasn't going to be able to turn Billy in, and you took off for the woods with my clue in your jacket, so I had to follow or be left out. But then you dropped the egg and I spotted it on the other side of the swamp."

"That was one slippery egg . . . I didn't know it was gone until I was pretty far away from it—I wasn't sure where I'd lost it," he explained.

"Up until that point, I was only a little suspicious. I opened the egg and discovered the message in code. Of course, you knew how to write secret messages and so does Billy and even Bernard-the-weasel. In fact, I'm probably the only person in the whole school who can't," she said sadly, remembering her grandfather's shocked expression when he saw the tin full of bald cupcakes.

"I was rinsing my shoes when I heard a scream. I looked up to see you fighting the rapids for your life. I raced across the woods to the other side, where I hoped to pull you out . . . only I wasn't strong enough. Just when I thought I couldn't hold on any more, Billy appeared out of nowhere and helped. That proved Billy had been following me all along."

Taking the last sip from his cup, Temple grinned. "So, it was Billy all along."

Erin's expression didn't change. "You know, Temple, it's a good thing Billy was following us. Things might have turned out differently if he hadn't."

She leaned in toward her friend. Temple's eyes stared back.

"Billy wasn't the person sending me the clues," she whispered.

"What? Of course he was," Temple replied anxiously. "You've just proven it."

"No; Billy was only there to solve the mystery, just like us."

A glint appeared in Temple's eyes, and he finally nodded. "I know . . . he came to see me at the hospital, and we had a long chat. You're right . . . he was following us. Seems after you accused him in school, he decided to catch the mystery person himself. Do you know he even followed us into the mine? How we missed him I don't know, but it's a good thing he wasn't hurt. You know, Rinny, Billy isn't so bad. I kinda like him . . . I think he'll make a good president."

"I think he will too," she said in agreement.

Temple propped his leg up and leaned back against his seat. "Then . . . who was the person sending the clues, if it wasn't Billy Perez?"

"The most important clues had been there the entire time, but it wasn't until I broke the code that I knew for sure," she said, placing the message on top of the wicker table.

"You broke the code?" asked Temple skeptically. "That must have been hard."

"You can learn anything at the library. I took out every book I could find on deciphering. It took me awhile, but it was really quite simple once I figured out what the person had done."

"Smart girl," Temple said. "You didn't mess around. So how was it encrypted? A Caesar Alphabet? An undivided cryptogram? A Nihilist transposition?"

She pointed to the message:

Hrleteatleap Brhatehrh
eeishlscu Hpyitdyh Cuc

"First, I tried using the alphabet to break the code. I went forward one letter, back one letter, forward two letters, back two letters, but no matter how I tried to substitute letters, it didn't make any sense."

"I can see that from just looking at it," said Temple, bent over.

"Of course you can. You're an expert . . . but I couldn't see it right away. It's kind of like the magic eye pictures. At first you can't see it, but then it becomes really easy, once you've trained yourself. This code is the same way." She leaned back and folded her arms.

"So, Miss Genius, what does it say?" he asked.

"It says, 'Meet me at McDonald's for the chicken nugget special. Midnight. Come alone,'" she whispered in low, hushed tones.

Temple sat up and frowned. "Don't make me get ugly. Now, what does it really say?"

"Be patient," she scolded at first. Then she broke into a wide grin. "See, the entire message wasn't in the same code. There was a stumbling block, just in case I figured it out too soon. And it wasn't meant to be broken early. You see, this morning, on my birthday, I was finally able to read the message."

Temple moved in closer. "Well?"

"Look," she said, pointing to the paper. "Start with the first letter on top." She placed her first finger on the letter "H" and then dropped it down to the first letter of the bottom line, the "e." Then she moved up to the "r" in the top row. Then she went down to the second letter in the bottom line, the "e".

Hrleteatleap Brhatehrh
eeishlscu Hpyitdyh Cuc

"See, 'H-e-r-e' is the first word. The letters represented themselves, meaning "a" was really "a," and "b" was really "b." And that can be tricky in a code, because the first thing you assume is that the letters mean something else."

"That's true," added Temple.

"The difference was in the way the letters were spaced. You couldn't read it like a regular sentence, going from the left side to the right. You had to go back and forth between the lines taking one letter at a time from each and adding it to the letter in the other row. "The first word was 'here,' the next word was 'lies,' and the next word, 'the.' When you connect all the words it says, 'Here lies the last clue, Happy Birthday, the Church.' "

"Wow . . . that's really strange," murmured Temple, his hand stroking his chin.

"See, most of the clue was written exactly the way it was to be read," she informed him proudly. "But not, 'the Church.' 'The Church' is not the whole congregation of my church as one might suspect; it is a person's name. Once I realized that, and I didn't know anyone called 'the Church,' I realized 'the Church' was a synonym, you know, a word having the same meaning as another word. This person didn't want to be discovered right away. In school, we turn all our spelling words into synonyms, so this wasn't so hard."

"Really?" said Temple. "It might have stumped me. I know at least three guys named Church." He laughed heartily, totally amused with himself.

Erin returned the paper to the pink egg and placed it among the other birthday gifts. "Thank you, Temple," she said affectionately. "It was great fun."

"Thank you for what?" he asked, inquisitively.

"Thank you, " she said, squeezing his hand, "for giving me a mystery for my birthday. Only you would think of something that cool. See, the word church is a synonym for the word temple, a place of worship just like a church. *Here lies the last clue, Happy Birthday, Temple.*"

Temple cheered. "You did it, Lady Erin . . . you figured it out. I thought when Billy Perez started following us, it would ruin everything, but it only made things better. He followed me into the woods, after watching me slip the egg into the general's hat, and confronted me. I told

182

him all about the mine and old lady Haggerty. He made me repeat the part with the ladyfingers. I was just finishing the story, when you walked up the riverbank in such a disaster. We had never seen anyone so covered in mud and acting so miserable. We couldn't stop laughing!" he said, clapping his hands. "That's when I fell in. You really are a clever girl."

Erin looked at him, surprised.

"So, what made you so sure it wasn't Billy?" he asked.

"Because Billy was taking the presidential race seriously. He wouldn't have risked being caught in a game of clues . . . and when I thought about it, you were there every time I found a clue. The rat appeared after you arrived . . . both you and the box were waiting for me on the porch . . . and you didn't want me to examine the wax on the mysterious box, because it was stamped with a 'B.' 'B' as in 'Black,' your last name. It was only a coincidence that Billy's name started with a 'B.' Then you showed up at the mine with a burglary set," she said, confidently. "And who finds the locket? You! Billy wouldn't have known about it. And you've always been obsessed with the Haggerty mansion, dreaming of hidden treasure and midnight ghosts."

"Excellent detective work, Erin. I had the time of my life," declared Temple with a chuckle. "Well . . . except for the bit with the river and meeting old maid Haggerty. I can live without seeing her again."

"Me, too," giggled Erin. "Although, Winston was nice."

"True." Temple patted his stomach approvingly.

"Temple . . . you've called me 'Erin' twice today," she stated, in a more serious tone.

"Really? Isn't that your name?" he asked. "You haven't changed it, have you? I mean, you haven't taken on another identity for a birthday present or something like that?"

Erin nodded to herself as if an important decision had just been made. "No, my name is still Erin. But, Rinny is your special name for me and always will be," she said softly. "I give you permission to use it."

Temple grinned with satisfaction.

Erin crossed her arms and looked toward the kitchen, where the noise level had risen. "We still have a mystery you know."

"And what is that, M'Lady?" he asked, bowing royally at the waist.

"The mystery of the missing miners . . . If I'm not mistaken, you never did find the solution." Passing Temple his crutches she continued, "I've been thinking about it, but first we have to eat, because I don't want Uncle Lonnie to gobble up all the ribs."

Then they stepped through the dining-room door to celebrate the end of the adventure with a magnificent feast.

About the Author

Robyn Leslie was born in Honolulu, Hawaii, but her life as an islander only lasted two years. Growing up in Ohio, she explored the great outdoors, invented games to play with her friends, and read all the good children's books. And like many young girls, it was detective *Nancy Drew* who instilled in her a love for mystery. This love for mystery was recreated in one of her favorites games, the "Trail of Clues", where the player was presented with a series of challenges. When relocation to England presented her with an opportunity to join an eclectic group of master writers, it was with their guidance she honed the craft of storytelling. She later returned to the States with a newfound passion for the magical world of fiction, and *Rinny and The Trail of Clues* was born.

Ms. Leslie is a teacher at an award-winning school in northern Florida, where she lives with her husband, daughter, and two mischievous cats.